D1122770

Hockey Player For Life

Howard Shapiro

iUniverse, Inc.
New York Bloomington

Hockey Player For Life

iUniverse books may be ordered through booksellers or by contacting:

iUniverse
1663 Liberty Drive
Bloomington, IN 47403
www.iuniverse.com
1-800-Authors (1-800-288-4677)

ISBN: 978-0-595-51785-5 (pbk)
ISBN: 978-0-595-62031-9 (ebk)

Printed in the United States of America

Foreword

Do you remember the first time you pulled on skates, better yet the first time you played ice hockey on skates. Tell me you don't remember cold nights in the school yard, whether it was on ice or just running around chasing a ball with your buddies and knowing time was drawing near as the street lights were getting ready to turn on. I am often asked how difficult was it when I was no longer able to play hockey at the highest level and my response quite simply is; I miss playing the game, but as long as I am around the game in some capacity I am happy and content.

Why? Well, wasn't the reason you played growing up because you just loved the game. Being with friends and family, playing in tournaments or in the backyard. It always comes back to the memories that were created a long time ago and the desire to not only carry them on for yourself, but for your children as well.

Thank you Howard for bringing the game back to a place where we find the true meaning and sense of what the game of hockey has provided for all of us. An inner joy and comfort that can never be replaced or forgotten

Keith Primeau

Acknowledgments

Thanks to all of my friends at BD&E, Todd Erkel, Dave Borland and Lee Averback, Borders stores, Joseph Beth Booksellers, Val King (you are the absolute best!) and Chapters Canada, Cindy Himes, George Birman and the entire Pittsburgh Penguins organization, Tanya Mruck, Nancy Gilks, (the great) Jimmy Holmstrom, Jody Vance and the entire Toronto Maple Leafs organization, Renee Aiken, David Terry/AQUEDUCT, Lyle Hysen, Stan Lee, Bob Kane, Kathy Cochrane, Jeff Jones, Gary Craig, Kenny Greer, Alan and Terry Robinson, Ernie the dog, Joel Bloom (and Carmel), the Catanzarite Family, James Murphy and Kevin Greenstein, Dave Hanson, Greg Anzelc and everyone at USA Hockey, #27 Shawn Irwin, Joe Pietaro, Stan Savran and everyone at FSN Pittsburgh, Ellis Cannon and Digby, Joe Starkey, Scott Morrison and Hockey Night in Canada and Jeff Mauro and every member, parent, booster, or fan of the Churchill Chargers hockey organization (1971-1986).

Mighty thanks to my "interweb"/blogsphere friends: Lyle Richardson, Kat Kealy, Alec Brownscombe, Alin Mateescu, Erin Nicks, Jim Dwyer, Navin Vaswani, Shawn Gates, Jon Jordan, Trevor Alexander, Michael Dell and Matt Fenwick. Thank you all so much for helping me out. Please check out each of their hockey blogs!

Very special thanks to this group without whom this book would not have been possible: first and foremost Simon Cox for his creativity, vision, hard work and passion in designing this book. You did a phenomenal job, Simon! Nico DiMattia for the way cool speed painting video he did for me…thanks Nico! Steve Dora for his friendship and amazing design efforts…thanks for making me look good…again! Craig Baird, Kirill Kniazev,

Dave McColl, Brian Gillam, Lizanne Gray, Jarrett Gray and Joe Pelletier…all of you helped me so much and I thank you all for your time, support and input…it couldn't have been done without you!

Very, very special thanks to my great contributors who I am honored to have as part of this book: Keith Primeau thank you for the amazing job you did on the Foreword and Brian Kennedy and John Buccigross thank you both so much for contributing your quotes to the back cover. All three of you were so giving of your time and I will always be indebted and thankful to have your vital contributions.

Extra special thanks to my good friend Tom Cochrane (great songwriter, great performer, great friend and even better human being), Pete Townshend, Bob Dylan and Bruce Springsteen whose songs inspired my writing. I referenced over 25 Bruce Springsteen songs, places in his songs, and characters from his songs in this book and those references are a very small way of saying thank you to him from the bottom of my heart for his music and performances over the years. My sister Jody Shapiro and my mom Alice Shapiro for whom I could never write enough or say thank you enough for everything…I love you so very much.

Extra, very special thanks to Gina, Sasha and Nikita, I love you three more than anything in the world. Thanks for putting up with the long nights at the computer and for being away from home while I try to run down my dream.

This book is dedicated to the loving and everlasting memory of my Dad, Arnold Shapiro. While I can't remember any of my "illustrious" three goals from my ice hockey career, I do remember, like it just happened yesterday, the hockey times I shared with my Dad. Whether it was him breaking land speed records to make it to one of my games after he worked overtime (and me being so happy to see him walk in that I gave him a high five "through" the glass) or him taking me to my first Penguin game (vs. the California Golden Seals October 28, 1972), those very fond memories I will always cherish. But the time I remember most fondly was when the Penguins traded up to draft Marc Andre Fleury in the 2003 NHL draft. After it was announced that they had made a deal with Florida so they could move up from picking third to picking first, I tried three times to call him and got a busy signal each time because those same three times he was trying to call me and tell me the same news.

And that is what I miss most of all, simply talking to him and hearing his voice everyday. So, if you've read this far, please take a moment and pick up the phone and call your dad (or any loved one for that matter) and tell them how you feel about them. I wish more than anything in this world that I still had the opportunity to do that with my Dad.

"Vos es requiro quod EGO diligo vos meus bonus amicus."

Hockey Player For Life, A Supersonic Storybook Production, was filmed on location in Pittsburgh, PA, Trail, British Columbia Canada, Orlando, FL, Cordoba, Argentina, Pasadena, CA, Bristol, CT and Toronto, Ontario Canada

For more information please log onto www.howardshapiro.net please send your comments, questions or feedback to howard.shapiro@hotmail.com Please check out my page on myspace at http://www.myspace.com/howardshapiro or my book videos on www.youtube.com

Chapter 1
Remembrance

"It was twenty years ago today…" and it was for a very good reason I couldn't get that lyric out of my head. On this cold day after Christmas, my old AA hockey team, the East Slade Magic Rats, was holding a reunion game. It was the twentieth anniversary of our league and state championship season. Even though we won both championships that year, it was events that happened off the ice that season that meant more to me than what happened on the ice. It was those lessons I learned just preceding and during the championship season, which still affect me to this very day. It all started in the late winter, a few months before my thirteenth birthday. As I lean back in my chair, it seems like only yesterday as I think back to the mid-80's, a time of mullets, Jordache jeans and skinny ties.

I was a crazy, sick rock star back then. Well, a young rock star, in a small East Slade, Pennsylvania sort of way. You know how some communities or small towns lose their mind over football or basketball? Well, in East Slade, hockey ruled. Oh, the people here loved the high school football team and we had a decent basketball team too, but hockey was king around here. The high school team had won four state championships in the last twelve years and a good portion of the town came to all of the home games and traveled to the away games. All of the games were broadcast on local radio, some games were televised on the cable access channel and the town newspaper had a sportswriter, Rick Dunn, assigned specifically to the team. Suffice to say; while Detroit may be Hockeytown, East Slade could be named Hockeyville.

So, what made me a rock star? I was the can't miss kid, a "slick-skating defenseman, who can jump easily into the offensive zone. Indeed, Tom Leonard can score from almost anywhere on the ice." That was what Rick Dunn had written once and to be honest, it sounded really cool! The old dudes in town told me that I reminded them of Bobby Orr, the slightly younger, old dudes told me that I was like a young Mark Howe and the twenty-something dudes said I was like Paul Coffey, an honor to say the least to be compared with any of these men. Man, they all told me that I was going to be the first overall draft pick in the NHL draft one day and sign a contract for a ton of money. At least, that was what everyone thought and told me, except my coach. No, to Coach Brantford I could do almost nothing right. He told me that I didn't play tough enough, I didn't hit anybody and that my skating and passing needed a lot of work. If you came to a practice or a game you'd have never known that I scored 25 goals and had 39 assists what with Coach Brantford always harping on me about *something* I was doing wrong.

My dad would say, "Coach is right, if he says it and believes it, you should too." He told me how Coach Brantford's dad was his coach when he played for the Magic Rats, back in the day, and how much of a legend he was in town. He said that if he was half as knowledgeable about hockey as his dad was, then he would help me take my game to the next level.

We had just played in a tournament up in Etobicoke, Ontario and finished second out of sixteen teams. It was a great team effort as the Canadian teams and the team from Detroit were all tough. I was fortunate enough to have won the tournament MVP and a guy had come up to my dad afterwards and talked to him about me playing for the Toronto Red Raiders AAA team. He told dad that the Red Raiders were more or less an all-star team that played in tournaments in the spring and summer. The only problem would be that I would have to travel back and forth between Toronto and East Slade on weekends in the spring and early summer to practice and then play in the tournaments and this would interfere with my Magic Rats practices and games. Dad told me that it was my decision to make and he would support me no matter what I decided.

Getting my mom's support, I thought, would be a little trickier. She would tell me how proud she was of my accomplishments but she was always quick to remind me that if my schoolwork suffered because of hockey, then I wouldn't be playing hockey. It was as simple as that.

She could be pretty tough on me when it came to schoolwork. I used to think that was because I was an only child and she just had me to focus on. Although, I later learned that her mother, my grandmother, was a high school English teacher and she was tough on her when she was growing up.

That's not to say that my mom didn't have a fun side. Every Halloween she would make a costume and wear it while she handed out candy. She also organized a block party every summer. She'd cook this huge feast and then set up tables and chairs in our garage and call it "Alice's

Restaurant." All of the neighbors would stop by and it was fun helping her set up and serve the food.

On the drive home and over the next few days all I could think about was whether to accept the invitation from the Red Raiders to play on their team. I would have said yes in one second to the Red Raiders coach but I kept thinking that if I did go to Toronto, that I would be letting the guys on the Magic Rats down.

Dad called and talked to Coach Brantford a few days after we got back from the tournament and the coach seemed a little angry about me leaving in the latter part of the season, but he never came right out and said that. Deep down I wanted the coach to say for me not to go because he needed me, but that simply wasn't Coach Brantford's style. He was very consistent; if someone wasn't at a practice or game they might as well have not even existed because the coach would tell us that he was only concerned with who was on the ice that particular day.

I was worried how the guys on the team would treat me and if they'd be mad at me. Not just mad for a day or two, but if they would have a long term grudge against me if I left the team. The main guy I was concerned about was my fellow defenseman and nemesis "Wild" Billy Horton. Billy wasn't the best skater, shooter, passer, or defender but he made up for his lack of skill with an almost insane competitive spirit.

We had practice on Sunday nights and I wanted to let Coach Brantford and the guys on the team know what I was going to do. I hadn't even mentioned the invitation to anyone because I knew they'd try and get me to turn it down. I really wanted to go but I guess I was looking for a sign that playing for the Red Raiders was the thing to do.

As I lay in bed before leaving for practice, I looked over on my wall and saw the collage of hockey players I did when I was six-years-old for art class. Next to that was a Pittsburgh Penguins pennant and below that was a poster of Wayne Gretzky. It was this really cool photo of him on a pond standing by a net with his Edmonton Oilers jersey on. I was staring at that poster in a trance-like state until I heard, "Tom! Tom!" my dad was saying loudly. "Didn't you know I've been standing here?"

"Sorry dad, I didn't know you were there," I said slowly, still in a trance-like state.

"Didn't you hear me calling you before?" he asked.

"No, I didn't," I said.

"Well, are you ready to go?" he asked.

"Oh, yeeeeaaaah," I said with a big smile. "I'm really, really ready to go."

Chapter 2
Resistance

When I was growing up, playing hockey was what I thought about when I woke up and when I closed my eyes to go to sleep. I was still thinking about hockey hoping I would have a dream that involved the game.

Some evenings after I'd get my homework done and if there wasn't a game on television, I'd ask my mom to pull her car out of the garage and I'd go down there and get out my street hockey stick and Mylec orange ball and shoot it into the garage door. Not just shoot it anywhere into the door, but into the "net" I spray-painted. Most of the time I'd throw in, "Leonard walks around the defense, comes in on the goal and HE SHOOTS AND SCORES!" Or I'd add something about how that goal was scored in overtime of the seventh game of the Stanley Cup and now the Penguins or the Maple Leafs, my two favorite teams, were now the Stanley Cup Champions.

One time I did this and my friend and teammate, Frankie Jones had come over to my house to see me and he was standing at our front door and he heard my whole "call" and he proceeded to ridicule me about that for a month. I remember saying to him, "Like you've never counted down three, two, one, he scores." He, of course, said, "No way, I've never done that..." Yeah, right, what a liar! *Everyone* who has ever picked up a hockey stick or shot a basketball does that at one time or another.

So, it was hockey 24-7 for me. On weekend afternoons we'd have a pick up street hockey game underneath Abram's Bridge and then after dinner Frankie or another friend of mine from the team, John Rowan, would come over to my house or I'd go over to one of their houses and we'd watch the Penguin game or whoever else might be playing on television. I loved it all, those were my hockey days.

Even though Coach Brantford was a young guy, he was 24 years old, he had an old school mentality. He probably got that from his dad. My dad had told me that old Coach Brantford instructed his team that if an opponent went into the corner that they should be hit there and hit hard. Dad told me once how he got screamed at because he let an opponent skate out of a corner and take a shot on goal. "Stuart Leonard, Stuart Leonard, if number 10 comes out of the corner like that again on you, I will sit you down for the rest of the season!" Coach Brantford yelled. "Hit 'em hard!! I want to see you hit him so hard that the CCM from his helmet is etched in the glass!"

Coach Brantford told us that we should hate our opponents because they were standing in our way from reaching our goal. He'd say this before every game and a lot of the guys bought into that but I certainly did not. I just couldn't work up a hatred even for our biggest league rivals, the Colts Hill Crusaders. It just wasn't in me and probably never would be in me to have this deep seated hatred of someone, especially someone who played hockey. If you would have asked the coach if he'd like to have a team of players like me, skilled guys who could skate, pass and shoot, play hard but clean or a team full of players like Billy who weren't the most skilled but who would intimidate and attempt to put an opponent through the boards, he'd tell you in a nanosecond he'd want a team full of "Billys."

Billy and I had known each other for a few years as he and I first played against each other in a Dek Hockey league when we were eight years old. Billy lived over in Irondale which was on the other side of Abram's Bridge from us and that was the rough part of town. The guys who grew up there seemed to have a chip on their shoulder and his Dek Hockey team had a pretty bad rep. I remember hearing rumors about those guys, the Duke Street Kings. Separating what was rumor from the truth was difficult but these were the facts: they had one guy named Zero who was banned from the Dek Hockey center for inciting a brawl after he kicked a guy in the head. There was Taz who ran around like the Tasmanian Devil, swinging his stick around like a caveman would swing a club. And Billy himself had been suspended from the center for a month for punching an opponent and then challenging everyone on that team to a fight.

As we drove over to our first game against the Duke Street Kings my dad laughed and told me that, "The more things change, the more they stay the same." He was referring to how when he played street hockey back in the day there was a team from Irondale which included a "nine-foot" kid named Zambrano, a kid who was supposedly just let out of juvenile hall named Phil "The Animal" Kratowski and Billy's dad.

He told me Billy's dad, who was now the coach of Billy's team, was their goalie and back then he looked like a Volkswagen with a head and if you got near his crease he'd whack you in the back of the ankles with his stick. Dad said he was also constantly talking trash, so apparently the apple didn't fall far from the tree, as Billy never stopped talking trash in the time I had known him.

Billy and I had an uneasy alliance when we played for the Magic Rats. We were both defensemen so we worked together a lot in practice. While I was the better skater and passer, Billy was way more physical and he did have a good slap shot, although it wasn't the prettiest shot. He had a weird wind up and he would put every ounce of his very being into that shot. Coach Brantford used to say that he was, literally, trying to put the puck through the goalie.

I really admired and respected certain parts of his game. Traits such as his willingness to stand up for his teammates, his tenacity and his love of the game were all very admirable. I told him that once after a practice and he went off on me. He told me that I had to play tougher and be more physical in front of our net. He stopped short of calling me soft but I know that is what he thought deep down. I knew he was trying to make himself bigger by cutting off my legs, but in a way the competition between us made me want to be a better hockey player.

Chapter 3
Resentment
(and then some)

After I told my parents of my decision to accept the invitation to play for the Red Raiders got the response I figured I'd get from both of them. My dad was ecstatic and my mom simply wondered how long I'd have to be gone from home. I knew dad would be happy for a few reasons. First off, because he knew I loved playing hockey and going to Canada to play against great competition would make me a better player. I also knew he loved Canada and now he would get to spend a lot more time there. He used to joke with my mom that he wanted to retire to Canada, instead of moving to Florida like everyone else did. Mom would say to him, "Just check in every now and then," but she wasn't kidding.

I'll never forget what my dad said as we drove over the Peace Bridge towards Canada for the Etobicoke tournament. He said, "Tom, I'll tell you something I want you to always remember. Pretty much everything is cleverer in Canada." I didn't even know cleverer was a word but after traveling there a few times I had to agree with him. Everything was cleverer in Canada!

One of the first things I noticed was that there were Canadian flags everywhere! It seemed like every office building, shopping center and mall had a flag flying out front. It was kind of a shock for me to see that, since it seemed that the only time anyone put out a flag back home was on a holiday. Whether I was imaging it or not, the air seemed cleaner, the water tasted better and even the Heinz ketchup tasted better on hamburgers and fries in Canada.

I thought the best way to go about telling the guys I was going to play for the Red Raiders was to talk to them after practice in small groups. I did want to speak with Coach Brantford first, before practice. I figured that he wouldn't be surprised since my dad had already talked to him about the Red Raiders invitation. After he dropped me off at the rink for practice, I ran in and put my stuff down in the usual place which was between Frankie and my other friend Bobby Ramirez, we called him Bobby R. because we also had Bobby Greer who was Bobby G., and Bobby Heaton who was Bobby H. and all three played on a line together. We called them the Bobby's. I quickly said hi to them and a few of the other guys who were putting their gear on. Then I went straight to the back where Coach Brantford was sitting. He was talking with our assistant coach, Craig Malone.

"Hi Coach Brantford, Coach Malone," I said as I nodded at him. "Do you have a second?" I asked Coach Brantford.

"Yeah, sure, Tom. What's up?" he asked.

"I wanted to let you know that I decided to accept the invitation to play on the AAA Canadian team. It was a tough decision, but, I talked…" I said looking downward.

"Fine, I wish you the best up there," he said looking straight ahead, not at me.

"I discussed it with my dad and, he's, you know, alright with it," I mumbled.

"Tom, I said it was fine. We have a practice coming up that I need to prepare for right now. So, why don't you get ready even though you won't be part of the team."

"But, I want you to know that I'll do my best and hopefully I can help the team while I'm here and—"

"Tom, I need to focus on the practice and the guys who are here. So, if you want to practice then lets get ready, okay?" he said as he lifted his head and shot me a cold, hard stare.

"Sure, Coach Brantford. Um, well, um thanks."

Wow, that couldn't have gone any worse. I didn't expect him to go crazy with the kind words or encouragement, but a little of that would have been nice. I thought that he'd be mad at me because I wasn't going to be able to help the team in the stretch run. That was understandable but from a personal perspective, here was a chance for one of his players to better himself. Even though I wasn't expecting him to fall all over himself congratulating me and wishing me the best, I was hoping he would do just that.

I was taking my equipment out of the bag when Coach Brantford came in and he was walking toward the end of the locker room. He suddenly stopped and walked back to the center of the room. He slammed his stick down a few times on the floor and then said tersely, "Guy's, hold up a second." I looked around and saw all twenty guys on the team focus their attention on him.

"I wanted to let you know that Tom will not be playing in our remaining games. He's decided to accept an offer from a tournament team, a AAA team in Toronto, so he will not be playing anymore with us. While this is certainly a disappointment, and in some ways a large letdown on his part to you, each of you will have to make up for his absence. You'll be expected to raise your level of play, especially the defensemen and all of the members of the first power play unit. Since Tom just told me a few minutes ago, I have had to completely change up the drills I was planning to do this practice. I'd like the top two units and Michael at the front end of the rink. Gregg, I want you in Tom's spot on left, first D-unit, third and fourth units, plus Tom, you head down to the back end of the rink. Warm up first and then we'll get situated. Okay, let's move."

It was weird having all of the eyes on me. Actually it was very creepy. I did a slow turn and looked around the room at the guys and tried to quickly study their faces. Some of them gave me a half smile, others looked mad and the one who looked the most upset was Billy. I didn't want to squint, but I could have sworn I saw little puffs of smoke coming out of his ears.

I was way far behind the other guys getting my equipment on and as a few walked by me on their way to the ice, they tapped their stick against my pads. That was a nice gesture even if they were mad at me deep inside. Frankie told me congratulations and slapped me on the back, Bobby R. did the same and also told me, "Go get 'em." Billy walked by me and then came back, stopped and looked at me and said, "So, Leonard, going up to the big league, huh?"

"Yeah, I'm going to give it a shot," I said as I looked him straight in the eye.

"Well, good luck...you'll need it. They play for keeps up there and some pansy, wuss defenseman like you had better get ready to be pummeled. You better grow up fast, son, or you'll be in a world of trouble," he said.

"Thanks, Billy, I appreciate the advice. I like to think that if they can't catch me, they can't hit me," I shot back.

"Dream on, dude. They'll line you up and take you down, believe me," he snorted back.

"How do you know so much about AAA?" I asked. "Have you actually played a game up there? My guess is you were watching because you have to be invited to join a club."

"Keep dreaming, keep dreaming. You let every guy in here down by going up there and we won't ever forget that," he said as he stormed away.

He made his point. I would have to toughen up but the part that stung me was the comment about letting the guys down. That hurt because it was true, I was letting them down. The thought had crossed my mind before when I was thinking about the offer…maybe it was true that I was a bad guy, a self centered, me-first guy. Only one guy was left in the room and he was walking toward me.

Chapter 4
Relationship

Terry Adamson was that last guy in the room and I didn't really know him too well. I knew most of the guys on the team from playing with or against them in Mite and Pee Wee, but this was Terry's first year of organized hockey. He went to a different school than me and he was a quiet guy, both on and off the ice. At practices and games, he'd usually get dressed in a different part of the locker room and even then I never really talked to him. I don't know if anyone ever talked with him because he always had headphones on blaring music. Every now and then before practice or a game he'd have the headphones on and he always seemed to be listening very intensely.

I was tempted to ask him what he was listening to, but I didn't. When he'd sit there with his eyes closed, his shaggy, long brownish hair swinging side to side he looked like quite the rocker. He usually wore a concert T shirt to practices and games. The Stones, The Who, Springsteen, Dylan, and U2 were names I recognized, but some of the names I had never heard of like The Mr. T Experience, Social Distortion and Black Flag.

Terry was probably the worst player on the team, he tried hard but he really struggled to put it all together. The really funny, and very odd, thing about him was that he was able to skate backwards better than he was able to skate going forward. I used to think this was the equivalent of being able to spell onomatopoeia, but not being able to spell cat even if you were spotted the 'c' and the 'a'.

Since he could skate backwards very well, the coaches put him back on defense and once in a while, in practice, he'd play right wing. I didn't really play with or against him because he worked with the third and fourth line players while I worked with the first two lines. He only played in the games when it was a blow-out but he never complained or griped, he always seemed happy to be on the team.

Now he was standing in front of me as I was really hustling to try and get all of my equipment on, get my skates laced and put on my helmet so I could join the rest of the team on the ice. I knew he was in front of me and he was just standing there which made for a very uncomfortable 20 seconds until I said, "What's up, man."

He took out his mouth guard and said, "Hey, I just wanted to say that is so cool that you're going to play for a AAA team in Toronto. I mean that is seriously cool."

"Thanks, I really appreciate that," I said as I continued to lace my skates in a furious manner.

"I mean, Canada, that's hockey heaven up there. Lemieux, Gretzky, Coffey, the Habs, the Leafs…I just think it's great that you're headed up there. Maybe this will help you get a college scholarship or maybe a pro scout will see you and—" Terry said excitedly.

"Whoa, whoa. I've never even stepped on the ice with those guys. The coach invited me to join but I have no idea how things will shake out up there," I said as I kept lacing up my skates. "I don't know how I'll fit in. Stuff like that is running through my head."

"Oh you'll do fine," he said excitedly. "I mean, you have it all going on, man. My guess is that you'll play on the PK and be a top four D, no doubt—"

"I don't know, we'll see I guess," I said shrugging my shoulders.

"When do you start, when's your first game?" he asked.

"Actually, there are practices next weekend and the weekend after that is the Markham tournament. The weekend after that is the Oakville tournament, I think."

"Oakville, hmmm, Vic Hadfield came from Oakville."

"Vic Hadfield…?" I said quizzically.

"Yeah, uh, he played left wing. He played for the Rangers and the Pens," Terry said proudly.

"How do you know that?" I asked incredulously.

"Oh, I follow the NHL super closely. Don't you? Plus, I collect cards, too. I have tons of them! I seem to always get those guys whose card you have doubles and triples of, you know. Getting a Lemieux or Gretzky card is like next to impossible but you'll pull a Tony Tanti, a Tom Fergus or a Lucien DeBlois card each pack. You know, guys who are decent players but not superstars by any—"

"Do you two care to join us or would you like to carry on your conversation down at McDonald's?" Coach Malone said as he walked into the locker room.

"Sorry coach, I'll be out in a second," I said as I flung my white jersey over my head.

"Yeah coach, I'm sorry I'm on my way right now," Terry said as he walked towards the door. He stopped and turned around and said, "Congrats again, Tom. That's really cool and I know you'll do well. Maybe I'll talk to you some more later."

"Yeah sure...we can talk later," I said as I put my helmet on and snapped the chin strap.

I walked out of the locker room and then jumped onto the ice and started skating around as the rest of the team was doing. I couldn't help but think how cool that was of Terry to say such nice things. That was more then either of us had ever said to the other and it made me feel good. That feeling, though, would be short lived.

Chapter 5
Retribution
(Part 1)

I always loved the sounds you'd hear at a practice. The silence in the cold rink, no one in the stands and then as the guys skated around you hear the blades crunching into the ice. When I would step on the ice for a practice, game or even a public skate the second I heard that sound of ice meeting metal I'd smile. Actually, I would take in all of the sounds and smells and the rink we practiced and played at was a special place to me in my formative hockey days.

The rink was named the Fairview Ice Garden. Fairview was a little borough located about ten minutes from East Slade. The rink itself was located at the end of a long, winding road and from there it looked like a big barn, not an ice rink. There wasn't even a sign or a message board or anything that said *Fairview Ice Garden* and it really had seen its better days. It had been built in the 1960s and because of some of the teams and games that were played there back in the day, Fairview was legendary. It was too bad that the owner had let it get run down, making it kind of a mess inside and out. Freezing, I mean arctic cold, inside with tiny locker rooms and a parking lot that looked like a bomb exploded in it gave people reason to call it "Crapview." Even so, the character of the place was still present.

Championship banners of Pee Wee, AA and high school teams hung from the low ceiling and jerseys of some of those teams were in the very, very large cases they had in the lobby. Combine that with uneven ice and boards covered in thousands of black puck marks and you have, to me, a hockey landmark. We'd fill the place up during our games and when people started yelling and cheering loudly it felt like the roof was going to fly off. Some of the teams we'd go up against played in newer rinks that were popping up all over the area, but I always felt that Fairview was our little Madison Square Garden or Maple Leaf Gardens.

Coach Brantford blew the whistle and yelled for the first and second line along with the first and second defense and Michael, our starting goalie, to head to the front-end of the rink and everyone else to the back end. Coach Brantford would always work with the first and second units and Coach Malone worked with the other guys. Then with about 15 minutes left to go in the practice we would scrimmage. It had been that way since the beginning of the year. I used to think that Coach Brantford didn't even know the names of the guys on the third and fourth units and I was positive he didn't know our back up goalie's name was Brian since he called him Brad.

However, and for whatever reason I'll never know for sure, Coach Brantford skated by me headed to the far end of the rink like a house on fire. A bunch of us were standing around, kind of in shock, because he was going to work with the third and fourth units. Though we were still in shock about what was going on, we hustled up and skated quickly to the far goal where the coach was.

"Come on, let's go," Coach Brantford bellowed. "We're going to run a three-on-one drill for shifts of a minute and half each. I want Ricky's line to go up against Tom and then Jack. Then Reese, your line will go up against Terry and then John Rowan. If the line scores, take the puck outside the blue line and start again. Defensemen, your goal is to get the puck outside the blue line, skate it to the blue line."

This was the first time we ran a three-on-one drill like this all year. Usually we would do skating or shooting drills or work on breakouts first, so this was different for sure. I was up against center Ricky Mason's line which had Eric Oswald on left wing and Larry Nicholson on right wing. All three of those guys shot left handed like me. They were solid, not spectacular players who did a good job for the team when called upon. Ricky would move up to the second line occasionally and each guy had probably scored three or four goals this year. They didn't see too much ice time as Coach Brantford normally used only two lines and he'd only throw the third line on when the period was about to end or if the game became a blow out.

Ricky had the puck just outside of the blue line as I set up in between the two circles near Brian. Coach Brantford passed the puck to Ricky and blew his whistle. Ricky skated inside the blue line and passed the puck over to Eric. He and Ricky then criss-crossed and Eric then skated from the right side toward the middle headed straight at me. I was skating slightly backward and then I stopped as Eric was headed right towards me. Eric then passed the puck to his left to Larry. I took two strides and reached as far as I could with my stick in my right hand to block the pass. I was able to do that and Larry came to a quick skate stop and he gave chase to the loose puck as did Eric. I raced toward the puck as well. As Larry closed in from my right and Eric came flying across from my left. I reached with both hands on the stick to lift the puck up in the air and I did a spin to avoid Eric as he was reaching for the puck and he went sailing into Larry. Those two crashed into each other and I had momentum coming off my spin and the puck hit the ice and I was able to pick it up. I looked back to see where Ricky was. He was over in the corner so I knew I now had smooth sailing to the blue line. As I turned around to face forward—

BOOM! I remember hearing the guys gasp or yell "Whoa." It felt like I hit a brick wall as my stick went flying out of my hands and the puck dribbled slowly across the blue line. I shook my head and looked up and saw Coach Brantford standing above me. He reached down and pulled me up by my right elbow.

"You okay?" he asked me.

"Um, yeah, I guess," I said slowly.

"You were skating without looking forward. I just stepped in front of you," he said.

"I didn't know you were in the drill, coach," I said.

"You have to be ready to take a hit. You have to have your head and face forward or someone will come over and light you up. If you had your head up you would have seen me, but you didn't and if you do that up in Canada you WILL get hurt. Up there, they'll be looking to separate your head from your shoulders. I'm only trying to help you," he stated very matter-of-factly before skating away and yelling to reset the drill, same line against Jack. I skated to the side boards and stood behind Terry, still a little bit groggy.

Terry turned around and said to me, "He, uh, just slid over to where you were going and stopped and you ran right into him ..."

"Whatever," I said angrily.

"You played that really good. You did the right thing driving Eric to the left knowing that he's a lefty that it would be hard for him to pass against the grain, you know, against his body to the left hash mark. Even though Larry was open and he could have done a one-timer if the pass made it through… the odds of that happening were slim. Plus, you made a nice move to tip the puck away and then that Spin-o-rama was too sweet, dude!" Terry said, all in one very long breath.

"You're giving me waaaay to much credit, man," I said as Ricky scored on a slap shot from just inside the left circle and Coach Brantford yelled for his line to set it up again. He also hollered at Jack to get ready. "Eric just went to his left, I didn't drive him there. He must have thought that he could get the puck to Larry."

"Well, it worked," he said.

"Except for coach putting me on my butt," I said.

We each started to laugh. I looked out and it looked like target practice on poor Brian. He was flopping to his right and then back to his left to try and prevent a goal. He made a good pad save and then he dropped down to his knees to cover the rebound but Eric poked it away. Jack whiffed on a clearing attempt and Larry had the puck and a wide open net and he buried the shot in there. Coach Brantford blew the whistle and yelled for Reese's line and Terry that they were up.

"Let's do it, man," I said to Terry as I tapped his shin guards.

He nodded back and skated out to just in front of the blue line. He had a kind of weird, choppy stride when he skated forward and he seemed to have great difficulty stopping. He tried to stop by curling in his left skate.

Terry was up against Reese Smith, Kelly Lucas and Jeff Craig who formed the fourth line. All three of those guys had not been playing hockey that long, but they all hustled and played hard when they got onto the ice. The thing I liked about them is that they were very supportive of the other guys and they played the game right when they did get the chance to play in a game. They never came out and tried to goon it up, which I admired and told them so.

Reese, a left-handed shooter, brought the puck in over the blue line and then quickly did a skate stop. Terry put on the brakes as well and then skated forward to pressure Reese who did a quick fake to Kelly on his right and then he passed the puck on his backhand over to Jeff who took the pass in stride. Terry, a right handed shooter, was skating forward as fast as his legs could take him. Reese quickly passed the puck over to Jeff. Terry tried to do a skate stop on his right skate, which he dug into the ice. However, he didn't dig his skate into the ice as much as he should have and he ended up making a semi-circle and then he stumbled forward and fell on the ice in front of Reese. Terry then struggled to get up as Jeff and Kelly skated in on a two on none break. Jeff came in on Brian, faked a shot, Brian went down face forward and then Jeff slid the puck over to Kelly who fired the puck into the wide-open net.

"Good job, guys…Kelly way to pick your spot, nice pass Jeff. Brad, you have to stay more upright. You played it right in that you have to take the shooter. Try not to go down as early as you do," Coach Brantford said and then he wound up with his stick and tapped *Brian* on his leg pads.

"Alright I want to work on breakouts. I want Ricky's line with John and Jack and then Reese's line with Tom and Terry. I want Ricky's line on offense and the goal for Reese's line is to get the puck out quickly. I want everyone on the blue line and at my whistle, after I shoot the puck in, I want the center and a winger fore checking, staying right on the puck. Take the body if you have to so as to gain control of the puck and hopefully get a scoring opportunity. On my whistle, let's go," he said.

We had done this drill many times before, although I was always paired up with my regular defensive partner David Stinson. I liked it because one of my strengths was rushing the puck and I could carry it or dish it off quickly and then even jump in the play. I looked over at Terry who was next to me at the blue line and I said, "Let me get the puck, even if it is in your corner."

"Okay, I'll set up in slot to try and clear anyone out. But, remember you'll have the two fore checkers on you so don't send it behind the cage to me cause I won't be there. You'll have to go up the wall," Terry said.

"Or, I can skate with it," I said.

"You won't have time to rag it, with the two guys on you the best bet is to go up the half wall. Don't go behind the net because I won't be there," Terry said as he motioned with his stick.

At that moment Coach Brantford blew the whistle and shot the puck softly into the left hand corner. I got a good start, ahead of everyone else, and as I picked up speed I was already thinking that I was going to get to the puck first and be able to skate it out. I looked over to my right and saw that Terry was skating backwards towards the slot, just like he said he would.

I was really impressed by his hockey knowledge and he seemed to have great instincts for the game, for reading the play. He wasn't the most talented player, but his knowledge of the game was first rate.

I got to the corner and the Coach had done a good job sending the puck in and it was just laying there. That may have been because the ice was uneven in that spot as it was in many spots at Fairview. That was also the corner where the Zamboni came out of so there were ruts in the ice. I had a second to look up and saw that Eric and Larry were coming fast so I grabbed the puck and skated behind the net. I looked up and Terry was in front of the net and I had Eric and Larry chasing me and Rick was guarding the right hand boards. Reese, Kelly and Jeff weren't much help as they were standing close together just inside the blue line.

I thought about passing the puck over to Terry but I had momentum and I thought I could beat Rick one-on-one so I skated towards him, dipped my left shoulder and he took the fake by moving to his right. I took a cross-over step and now I saw the center of the ice open as John and Jack were tied up by Kelly and Jeff. I skated right up the center when I heard Coach Brantford's whistle loud and clear. Everyone stopped and looked over at him. He yelled out, "Hold on!"

"Tom, what are you doing?" he screamed at me.

"Just trying to get the puck out," I said.

"Is it Tom versus everyone else?" he said loudly. "What about the other four players? Don't they count?"

"Sure, Coach, I just saw the opportunity to skate with the puck and it looked like the guys were tied up and—"

"You work with your teammates, you work with your defensive partner, and you play a team game. Once again, you try that maneuver in Canada and someone, I assure you, will take the puck away and then have an odd man break all because you didn't get rid of the puck."

"Sorry, Coach. It just seemed like the only play I had."

"Don't say you're sorry, just think twice before you think you can go one-on-five. And now give me ten laps, blue line to goal and back. When Tom's done we're going to switch sides."

So that's the way the practice was going to go, I thought. Instead of praising me for getting the puck out, I got hollered at and had to do ten laps. Plus, that was the second time the coach was telling me how my style of play wasn't going to fly when I started playing in Canada. What did he know about how they played up there, I thought, as I skated between the blue line and the goal line. I was invited because of the player I was and I had come pretty far on my ability and I had to be me; I wasn't going to change when I got up there.

Chapter 6
Regarding
(my departure and my so-called NHL dream, Part 1)

Surprisingly, the next portion of practice went okay. We did some drills and I got through without being pummeled either physically or verbally by Coach Brantford. I looked at the clock and we only had 15 minutes left to go in the practice, I was a little tired but I was hoping we'd still scrimmage. Knowing we were going to scrimmage made going through a rough practice a little easier and Coach Brantford put us through a bunch of tough ones. Especially early in the season, we'd work on breakouts and other passing drills over and over and over till our arms were almost too tired to lift.

"Alright, I want Stevie's line with Billy and Tim against Reese's line with Tom and Terry. Billy, you bring the puck up. Okay, let's go on my whistle," Coach Brantford said.

Throughout that year the top two lines and top two defensive pairings would go against each other for the majority of the scrimmage time. With just a few minutes left the third and fourth lines and defensive pairings would go against each other. At no time during that year did the number one or two lines or defensive pairings go up against the fourth line and I would easily have remembered that since I was on the first defensive pairing.

Making things even more unusual, at least to me, was the very private talk I saw Coach Brantford and Coach Malone having with just Billy at the far end. Even though my nose had been broken before, I smelled a rat.

"This will be cool, us going against the first line," Terry said as we stood on the blue line awaiting Coach Brantford's whistle.

"Yeah, it will be…it will be something," I said half-sarcastically.

"I love it, I've never gone against those guys," Terry said excitedly. He paused for a brief second and then without taking a breath launched into, "I'll tell you what to watch for. Stevie has trouble going to his left and Scott will always jump ahead on the wing so if you can force him to his left in the neutral zone, there's a good chance that he'll be offside. Frankie has trouble stopping on his left, sort of the opposite of me, and he'll sit along the half wall on the off wing just waiting for a one-timer opportunity. If you or I can force the puck back to Billy's side, he does that throwing-himself-into his slap shot routine and Eric or Rick could probably poke-check him and be off to the races. Michael is very beatable on the stick side up high—"

"Whoa, man, slow down!" I said to him as I shook my head. "First things first. How can you talk for so long without taking a breath? The main thing for us is that we've got to hold them off. Stevie may have trouble going to his left but he can darn well go forward a lot faster than just about anyone else in our league."

"No, that's cool…I mean you're right. We have to play smart down low, not try to get crazy with the puck, move it up to the wingers and I'll cover for you if you get the chance to carry the puck in," Terry said nervously.

Coach Brantford blew the whistle and Billy skated the puck over his blue line before passing over to Stevie. I kind of thought it was cute that Terry was so into the scrimmage. He was acting like we were in overtime in the seventh game of the Stanley Cup Final, not a scrimmage at the end of a practice. But that was fine because he didn't get to play much and I'm sure it was fun for him to be playing against the best players on the team. He knew a whole heck of a lot about our teammates and their various strengths, weaknesses and tendencies. It was almost like he was a coach or something.

Stevie got the pass from Billy and skated over the red line. He looked up and saw that all five of us were hanging back and he fired the puck into the left hand side of our zone. I looked over and saw Terry frantically skating backwards and when he went to turn around, he fell right on his butt. He struggled to get up and I saw Brian start to come out of the net and then he panicked and skated back to the goal. The puck hit with a loud thud in the corner and then just died there; we certainly didn't get a good bounce. The puck was just sitting there as Terry struggled vainly to get up and skate to the puck when both Stevie and Frankie skated by him. Reese and Jeff were standing still also, like their feet were in cement watching the play.

I gave some thought to try and out-skate Stevie and Frankie but if I didn't beat them to the corner and the puck, then the slot would be wide open. So, I hung back a bit, kept my eye on Scott and set up in front of the net. Stevie was first to the puck and he went behind the net and held the puck there waiting for me or Terry, who was now back in the action, to chase after him.

"I've got the front, Terry, go get Stevie," I yelled over to him. He paused for a second, looked over at me, told me to watch out as Billy was coming up fast and then took a step to his left and fell down…again.

This unintentionally worked out well as it caused a lot of traffic to form on the right side of the net and forced Stevie to come to my side. I made a move to poke check the puck when out of the corner of my eye I saw Billy coming up on me with his arms crossed, lunging to hit me. At the very last second, I stopped and Billy went flying by me, completely missing the hit on me. Stevie then deftly passed the puck to Scott who was standing in the middle of the circle. Scott then launched a wrist shot at the goal. Brian kicked his right leg out and blocked the shot but the rebound bounced right to Stevie who had an open net to shoot at. Here is where luck really came into play.

Stevie was a phenomenal player, a great skater who was that rare breed in that he scored as many goals as he set up. He led our team in both goals and assists and he was a year younger than most of us. He may have missed one or two open net opportunities all year. So, what does he do…he shoots it up and the puck bounced off the cross bar and hit the glass directly behind the net. Stevie yelled in anger and Brian had a look on his face like he just saw a three-headed alien fall from the sky.

Scott picked up the puck behind the net and tried a wrap around shot but he didn't have full control of the puck and it ended up sliding out towards the right point. I was jammed up with Frankie in front. Tim whipped a quick pass over to Billy who was wide open at the left point.

Billy took a second to settle the puck and then he began his famous wind up, his left hand slid up towards the blade of the stick and his head flew way up. I broke free from

Frankie and positioned myself in the high slot to try and block the shot. Reese beat me to the punch as he slid in front of Billy who was putting his very being into the slap shot. The shot hit off Reese's shin guards and caromed outside of our blue line.

Billy fell to one skate and I saw an opening so I skated full bore ahead and, zipping past him, I picked up the puck along the left side boards by the red line and I was off to the races…almost.

I saw Tim skating hard from the right side and behind him was Stevie, also coming up fast. I skated with everything I had, hoping to beat both Tim and Stevie to the middle. As I crossed the red line, then the blue, I skated as fast as I could all the while trying to control the bouncing puck. I heard the guys on the bench yelling "GO!" and Terry hollered, "Go up top, stick side."

I saw Tim closing in and at the circle I decided to make my move. I swung my head back and forth and I dipped my right shoulder as if I was headed to the middle and this caused Tim to hesitate just enough to put him out of the play. It was now me versus Michael.

I looked up at him as he came out of his net to cut down the angle. I opened up my right shoulder and leaned forward as if I was going to try a wrist shot and Michael bought the fake and lunged out at me. I then shifted the puck over to my backhand and with Michael completely out of position, I backhanded the puck into the open net.

I didn't celebrate the goal by throwing up my arms or pumping my fists or anything like that, although I was very excited and happy with the goal. I skated behind the net and as I was coming around here comes Billy, yet again, and he lowered his shoulder into me, thereby sending me against the boards.

"What are you doing?" I yelled at him as I got up.

"You got lucky, twice, pal," he snorted at me.

"What's your problem, man?" I barked as I skated up to him.

"No problem, here." he said as he stood his ground.

"Alright, break it up!" Coach Malone hollered as he stepped between us.

"Michael, don't over commit and Tim you have to do everything you can to slow him up. You've got to get a piece of him, even if you have to take a penalty," Coach Brantford said.

No nice goal, Tom or nice play or great job from either of the coaches. Coach Brantford then told everyone to head to the showers, practice was over. He reminded everyone that we had games over the next two weekends at Fairview against the Winston Bears next weekend and then both the Lynnwood Knights and Colts Hill Crusaders the weekend after that. He said that even though we only needed to win just one of the three games to lock up a playoff berth, it was important to win all three to give us momentum headed into the playoffs.

As we walked back to the locker room all three Bobby's and Tim congratulated me on the goal. I looked for Coach Brantford but he and Coach Malone were still on the ice having another private chat with Billy. Guess he didn't get the job done.

Chapter 7
Revise

I was taking my pads off as Billy walked by. Coach Malone and Coach Brantford followed behind him and they went back to their area of the locker room. Billy sat down and I glanced over at him quickly and he looked back at me and then turned away. He then started talking to Tim who was his defense partner and best friend on the team. I'd steal a glance every now and then and noticed that both of them would pause from talking to each other and look over at me.

Coach Brantford hollered for Billy to come back to where he was and Billy said he'd be back as soon as he took his skates off. Coach Brantford hollered back, "Leave them on and get back here, right now!"

I got out of my equipment quickly as I wanted to get out of the locker room and head home. It had been a grueling practice and at that point I just wanted to think about going up to Canada the next weekend to start playing with the Red Raiders.

I finished getting dressed, grabbed my bag and said goodbye to Frankie and Bobby R. as I made my way quickly towards the door. As I was walking towards the door I heard,

"Tom, hey Tom" and I looked back and it was Terry. He came running out with half of his equipment still on.

"Hey, Tom, great practice! Thanks for helping me out so much," Terry said excitedly.

"No problem, you did a good job and you helped me too," I replied.

"Get real! How can I possibly have helped you out?" he asked.

"Having you out there was like having another coach," I said. "I mean, you know hockey and you know stuff about the guys on this team that I had no clue about."

"Well, that's because I do a lot of sitting," he said with a laugh.

"Maybe so, but man, you know the game like no other guy I ever met," I said as I punched him in the arm. "Just keep working at it and you'll do fine. I gotta run, my dad's waiting for me."

"Cool, hey good luck in Canada and maybe we can check out a Pens game or a Stanley Cup playoff game when they start," he said.

"Yeah, sure, that would be fun. Just give me a call, my numbers on the—"

"The team roster page, sure I'll call you," he said quickly, barely taking a breath.

"That would be great cause I think this year there are so many teams that could win it all, you know. You start with the Oilers and then—"

"You're right…but I gotta run, just give me a call. See ya," I said as I slapped him on the back and then I turned and walked towards the front door.

"See ya, man. I'll call," Terry said.

I knew my dad would be waiting out front for me. Once in a while he would sneak into practice and watch a few minutes. The reason he had to sneak in is because Coach Brantford had a very strict policy of not letting parents watch practices. If he saw a parent watching a practice, he'd stop the practice, skate over and politely, but firmly, ask them to leave immediately. I could see his point, some of the parents could be pretty annoying. Billy's dad was a good example; he would "coach" from the stands yelling that we should pass the puck to Billy, let Billy skate the puck up and so on. My dad was a lot different. Then again, there was the whole sneaking into practice routine he'd go through. He'd watch from behind a door, peering out every few minutes. For a guy who's job was being an accountant, my dad would have been a pretty good detective or a spy!

One thing about my dad was that he did things his own way. Seriously, he would sit away from the other parents at the games and watch intently, maybe clap after we score but that was about it. He never raised his voice or yelled instructions to me, Coach Brantford or the referee, unlike other parents.

My dad was a smart guy in all ways. He knew just what to say when we won, as well as when we lost. His demeanor was no different if I played a good game or a bad game. The only time he had ever said something harsh to me was the time he told me after the Stockton Wings game this year that I was going to win the Lady Byng Trophy if I didn't start hitting someone.

"You don't have to rip his head off or put him through the boards," he said. "However, you do have to help your goalie out by clearing out the traffic from in front of the net."

"But we were winning by five goals and there was like a minute and a half left in the game," I answered back.

"Doesn't matter," he said. "You play the whole game from the opening whistle to the final buzzer. You play the game hard, you play it clean, you respect it and give it all you've got. You have a responsibility to keep the front of the net clear and you also have the responsibility to stick up for your teammates and you should have done something when that guy hit David from behind."

"I know, Coach said the same thing…" I said quietly.

"It's okay… just learn from it and come out the next game and do your best," he said with a smile.

It was nice that it was just the two of us driving up to Toronto for the first practice. As we drove and the daylight receded into darkness, I was really jacked up. It was fun to stay in a hotel and to see a different place as well as eating nothing but restaurant meals as opposed to my mom's chili and meat loaf. Still, I was a little nervous about fitting in with the other guys on the team and I was concerned how they would treat me since I was the new guy. Another unknown was how the Coach, Bryan Gilmour, would treat me. I thought that he couldn't possibly be any tougher then Coach Brantford. Little did I know, at the time, how very wrong I could be.

Chapter 8
Red faced and rattled

On our drive to the rink, the Nevin S. Kirk rink in Georgetown, Ontario, before the first practice, I didn't say much to my dad. I was thinking about practice and also about what was going on back home with the Magic Rats. I missed being with those guys and I wondered how Terry was doing. For someone that I never knew that well and hardly talked to, he turned out to be an excitable, yet very nice guy. Someone who I would like to hang out with at the rink and away from it as well.

As we pulled into the parking lot I was immediately impressed. The lot was clean and big with no potholes or massive craters like at Fairview. I got my gear and walked into the rink and I let out a loud "Woah!" as I looked around. The place was so clean that you could have probably eaten off the floors. There were two rinks and the message board said Red Raiders practice on rink two. My dad and I made our way to rink two and standing outside of the locker room was Coach Gilmour. Dad had remembered him from the Etobicoke tournament and he waved and then walked towards us. He was a short guy with small glasses, a military buzz cut and he was wearing a Toronto Maple Leafs jacket.

"Mr. Leonard, Tom, welcome. I take it you had no problems getting here," he said in a short clipped tone.

"Not at all, you gave us some great directions," dad said. "Please call me Stuart."

"Of course, but I prefer Mr. Leonard or sir," Coach Gilmour said in a very prim and proper way. "Well, you're here Tom because we think you have some great skills. We run a tight, and I'll even say a great, organ-i-zation, here. Practices are crisp, hard hitting and very challenging. Again, we think you'll be up to the task or we wouldn't have invited you. So, let's go inside the dressing room here and I'll introduce you to the team."

Coach Gilmour walked ahead of us and after he said dressing room, dad and I looked at each other as if to say, "Huh, dressing room?" I assumed that Canadians called the locker room the dressing room but to me, and dad as well, the dressing room was a place in Sears or JC Penney where you tried on clothes.

"Is it okay, coach, if I stay and watch practice?" dad asked as Coach Gilmour held the dressing room door open for me.

"Mr. Leonard, please address me as Coach Gilmour," he said abruptly. "Of course you can watch from the stands. However I do have a strict set of rules and regulations and failure to honor those rules and regulations will cause immediate dismissal from this facility. Please refrain from cheering, passing judgment or in any way shape or form making any comments during the practice. Do not try to communicate with your son, any other member of the team or coaching staff while practice is going on and no note taking is allowed. Will you please honor my rules and regulations and are we completely clear on my rules and regulations, sir?"

"Crystal…clear coach," my dad said quietly before quickly adding, "crystal clear Coach Gilmour."

"Very good. Thank you sir. Tom, please join me," Coach Gilmour said.

I started walking with him as I looked back at dad who shrugged his shoulders and threw out his hands. This was his nonverbal way of saying "whatever." As we were walking to the *dressing room* I was becoming anxious. I just wanted to get the formalities out of the way and get on the ice and get the practice started.

I was always a little shy when it came to meeting new people or being put in different situations. Although, it was a different story once I got on the ice. There I had the confidence to know that I could rush the puck in and possibly score from anywhere on the ice, just like Rick Dunn had written. It would be a little weird here in Canada, as I was the little fish in the great big sea as opposed to back home where it was the complete opposite.

As I walked into the dressing room my eyes were as big as saucers. The room was enormous, well lit, carpeted and each player had his own stall! It sure as heck beat the tiny benches and freezing cold temperatures at Fairview. The room was loud with the guys on the team getting dressed for practice.

"Okay, listen up," Coach Gilmour said loudly in his clipped tone that I was now getting used to.

He continued, "I want to take a second to introduce the newest member of the Red Raiders, on defense, Tom Leonard. Take a minute and introduce yourself to him, okay boys? Tom, here, is from East Lansing, Pennsylvania which is not too far from Pittsburgh or Philadelphia?" he asked me.

"Pittsburgh," I interjected looking straight at him.

"That's Pittsburgh, Coach Gilmour. Understand Tom?" he asked me as he stared squarely at me.

"So, that makes you a Penguins fan right?" he bellowed at me. I stood still and looked around and with all of the sets of eyes looking at me I couldn't even remember the question. I paused for a second and then tilted my head to the left. Coach Gilmour must have taken that as a yes because he then said, "Well, none of us Leafs fans will hold that against you!"

Would Coach Gilmour have made a good drill sergeant? Well yes he would. As a stand up comedian the answer was no but you couldn't tell that from the way the guys on the team were laughing. My guess was that Coach Gilmour was such a bruiser, that when he did crack a joke, or in this case, attempt to crack a joke, that people just laughed to make him happy.

He probably wouldn't have made a good geography teacher either as there was no East Lansing, Pennsylvania. But that was okay, I figured most guys there had only heard of Philadelphia because of the Flyers and Pittsburgh because of the Penguins.

After the laughing died down, the coach pointed to a stall and there was a white number 22 jersey and above that a piece of tape that had "Leonard" written across it. I sat down and got my equipment out. I looked to my right and nodded to the guy getting ready. He nodded back but did not say anything. Well, nice to meet you too, I thought. I looked over to my left and said "hey" to the guy there who had finished putting his equipment on.

"Hey, man. I'm Garth Scrutton," he said. "I'm a left winger, coach said you played D."

"Yeah, I'm a left D. At least that's where I played at back home," I said.

"The teams we'll play in the tournaments are tough. You know, the competition is really good up here," Garth said.

"Well, that's why I'm here," I said with a slight smile. "To be the man you have to beat the man like Ric—"

"Whooo, like Ric Flair says," Garth said excitedly.

"You got it! You a Flair fan too?" I asked.

"I am and also the Four Horsemen," he said.

"Very cool," I said with a big smile.

"Look, um, just a little bit of advice," Garth said quietly. "Coach Gilmour, and Coach Clemmons for that matter, are very organized in everything they do. Very disciplined and they expect the same out of us. Make sure you play your position; they are very big on staying in position."

"Oh, uh, okay," I said in a hushed tone. "If I get the chance, I like to rush the puck."

"You've been warned," Garth said sternly. "I'm just telling you what may have worked down in your league in the States may not fly up here."

"Okay…thanks for the tip," I said.

I hurried up and got my equipment on and joined the few guys who were on the ice. The only guy who had introduced himself was Garth. I had not met Coach Clemmons either. I looked into the stands and sitting in the back row was my dad. I wanted to wave but I didn't want to draw any attention to him or myself. Plus, he was a cool customer, he wouldn't have acknowledged the wave. It was kind of surprising to see a few other parents scattered throughout the rink. I was looking around, taking it all in as I skated around. The ice was great, no ruts and it was so smooth. It was quite a departure from the ice at Fairview.

A loud whistle blew and then Coach Gilmour, who was standing in the center ice circle said, "Alright, boys, everyone come on over here."

"We have this practice and one tomorrow and then the big Markham tournament. Any of you who have played in that tournament know that the competition is fierce. There will be 16 select teams, the best against the best. We finished fourth last year and I'd like to improve on that. I think we have the talent to compete for first place, but I need you guys to want it. We'll have the Oakville tournament the weekend after Markham and then we'll have a month for us to prep for the Ottawa tournament. As you know, the Ottawa tournament is very important to me personally, and also a great showcase for you and our community. We can't travel to Ottawa without significant showings at the Markham and Oakville tournaments, I won't let that happen. So, let's get our work in now and then show the teams in Markham what Red Raider hockey is all about!"

A bunch of guys started yelling, "Red Raiders" in unison and some other started slamming their sticks down on the ice. I wasn't sure what to do so I just started yelling "Red Raiders, Red Raiders, Red Raiders" until the tall guy next to me looked at me like I was insane.

"Forwards behind this net," Coach Gilmour said pointing with his stick to the net to the right. "Defensemen and goalies behind the other net for the Australian line drill. You'll go on my whistle"

Huh, I thought as I skated with the other defensemen and the two goalies. My mind started racing as I stood in line. Since apparently no one was going to tell me what I had to do, I turned around and asked the guy behind me, "What am I supposed to do?"

"Oh, yeah, you're the new guy…what you have to do is skate through the dots and jump over the blue and red lines all the way around the rink. Line up back here and then do it again."

"Sounds easy enough," I said.

"See how those legs feel after the fourth or fifth time around the rink," he said. "Last year after we came in next-to-last place at the Vaughn tournament we did this drill for, like, a half hour. Just around and around. And then one time last year a kid messed up on a drill and the coach punished us all at the end of practice by doing this drill until the Zamboni driver kicked us off the ice."

"Yeesh," I said.

"Your name's Tom? I'm Levon," he said as he tapped his stick against my shin guards.

"Hey, Levon, thanks for the info on the drill," I said.

"Sure thing. The guy in the front of our line is Noah, Matthew is behind him, Stefan is behind him and the guys behind me are Phillip and Pierre Davidoff. They're brothers."

I nodded at Phillip and Pierre. Pierre was the guy next to me who looked at me like I was insane when I was yelling Red Raiders. He was an unusually large kid who looked more like he was 17 than 13.

I watched the guys skating and all of them could really motor. While back at home we had one line, three guys, who could really skate fast, each of these guys was fast. I mean like warp factor seven fast. I became very rattled as I knew right then and there to succeed here in Canada I was going to have to raise my game not one, two or three levels. No, I was going to have to step it way, way up and do it at warp factor seven speed.

Chapter 9
Revitalized

I handled myself really well in that first practice as well as the second one too. The drills were as intense as the names that Coach Gilmour had for them: break the wall, kamikazee skate and steal, full out slam, Geraldton jam and Saskatchewan cycle. We'd skate for the first hour or so of the two hour practice and only then would pucks come out. It was tough, but I made it through without messing up at all, although the brothers Davidoff certainly made their share of mistakes and the team usually paid for those mistakes with extra skating at the end of practice. While this didn't sit well with some of the guys on the team, no one was crazy enough to confront Pierre.

The coaches were complimentary of me and I was getting along great with the guys on the team. Levon was becoming a good friend of mine as was Noah who was my defensive partner. I also became friends with a guy named Landon who was a center and Randall who was the only other guy from the USA. He was a huge Sabres fan from Buffalo.

It was fun to be spending so much time with my dad. We had a great time driving up and back together. The drive never seemed very long because he and I would talk hockey or what I was up to in school or who I was hanging around with and he'd joke around a lot too.

The only arguments were about what we'd listen or play on the radio. He brought along his Bruce Springsteen, Bob Dylan, Led Zeppelin and The Who tapes and he'd want to listen to them over and over. I didn't mind listening to them but he'd play the same stuff over and over again. That and what we'd watch on TV back at the hotel room sometimes became an argument. I'd flip through all of the channels and he kept saying stop at this channel or that channel.

Driving to the Markham tournament I didn't know how much, if any, playing time I'd get. There weren't first, second or third line or defensive combinations like there were for the Magic Rats. Coach Gilmour said at the second practice that how we did in the practice would determine which line combination would be considered the first line and first defensive pairing and so on. Noah and I both played well in practice but I didn't know if that would be good enough to earn us a lot of playing time or not.

In the end it all worked out well. The team did great, we won the tournament beating the Humber Valley Foxes seven to one in the final game. I teamed up with Noah mostly, but I also logged some powerplay time with Levon and I ended up getting two assists in the four games that we played. I was on the ice for a bunch of goals that were scored against us, but Coach Gilmour didn't holler or yell at me. He came over to me on the bench and patiently reminded me on two different occasions not to stray from my position and to look to pass the puck as opposed to trying to skate with it myself. Our best line, which consisted of Preston, Landon and Garth, skated circles around the competition. Those guys could pass and shoot. My dad said watching them reminded him of watching the Russians in the Olympics with their precise passing and insanely fast skating.

Upon returning home after that first tournament, I felt on top of the world. I couldn't wait to tell Terry about how things went and I also wanted to check with him and see how the Magic Rats had done over the weekend.

"Hey, Canada was so cool," I said to Terry on the phone the night me and my dad got back from Toronto. "We won the tournament and you would not believe how good those guys were."

"That's cool, man," Terry said in a dejected voice.

"What's the matter? You sound like you're down in the dumps," I said.

"We lost all three games and now we're out of the playoffs," he said in a hushed tone.

"What the heck happened?" I asked.

"I dunno, defensemen didn't stay in their lanes, the forwards were all coming back and crowding the net and it was just a mess. Worst games we've played all year," Terry said.

"What were the final scores?" I asked.

"Three to two in both the Winston and Lynnwood games and eight nothing in the Colts Hill game," Terry said, his voice trailing off at the end.

"Geez, eight nothing, the Coach must have gone ballistic after the game," I said.

"He was really, really mad at us. You know he has this long-standing beef with Coach Simpson from Colts Hill, right?" Terry stopped and then started up again. "From what I heard from Reese, Simpson's mother was the commissioner of their high school league back then and she made Coach Brantford's team forfeit all of their wins when he was a senior because they had three players from another school district on their team. Coach Brantford's team took the league to court and they ended up winning the case. But, apparently, Brantford still holds a grudge because they didn't shake hands before or after the game."

"What'd the coach say? Did he rip into anyone specifically?" I asked.

"He kind of singled out Michael, who was bad but he wasn't getting much help. We didn't clear anyone out from in front of the net. Billy took a bunch of dumb penalties and the Bobby's couldn't clear the puck out of our zone at all. He laid into David as well and even your name came up," he said.

"How so?" I asked.

"He was saying how just because you weren't there that that was no reason for us to fall apart," he said and then stopped for a second. Slowly, he started back up, "He then said that you were a traitor for leaving and that he couldn't believe that we didn't show up against Colts Hill with a playoff berth on the line. Especially after we got beat by Winston and Lynnwood."

"I'm not a traitor or a villain. You know that, right?" I pleaded to Terry.

"I know it, man. But some of the other guys…well, you know some of them just kind of follow the coach blindly. I mean, I know you're a good guy and we just got beat, bottom line. The coach was just letting off some steam. If anyone should have taken the blame it should have been him for not having a better game plan and for not making any in-game adjustments. Like there was the time—" Terry said before I interrupted him.

"I'm sorry, Terry, my mom needs to use the phone. Do you want to, uh, come over here and watch the Pens-Rangers game tomorrow night?" I asked him.

"Sure, that'd be great," he said excitedly.

"Cool. Let me call you back as soon as my mom's off the phone and I'll give you directions and stuff," I said.

"Awesome," he said before he hung up.

My mom didn't have to use the phone but if I would have stayed on with Terry I'd be on the phone for an hour or so. He knew hockey alright, but I didn't want to get a blow-by-blow list of reasons we lost those games. Plus, I was really disappointed that the coach would call me a traitor.

That wasn't fair or true, but then I started thinking later that night, what if Stevie or one of the other guys on the team missed a few crucial games to play for another team. Would I be mad at him or feel he let me and the other guys on the team down? The answer was yes. So, maybe deep down, maybe the coach was right. There was nothing that dictated that I go to Canada and play for the Red Raiders. Maybe I *was* putting my dreams and ambitions above the team's.

I was feeling very good about myself as I had a good tournament against top flight competition. Although, now I had half of my team, if not more, plus the coach mad at me and accusing me of being a traitor. There was only one person I knew who could help me make sense of all this.

Chapter 10
Rebound
(and then back down)

"So, now I'm Benedict Arnold in the eyes of Coach Brantford and who knows how many of the guys on the team," I said at breakfast the next day to dad.

"That's the way life goes sometimes," he said as he sipped some orange juice. "You and I both know that you're not a traitor. Don't sweat it, you have to focus your energy on this weekend's tournament in Oakville. One of the parents, I think it was Levon's dad, told me that Coach Gilmour was going to book an hour of ice time on Friday night, so we'll have to leave at noon on Friday."

"Cool!" I said with a huge smile.

"Yeah, I figured I'd have to twist your arm to get you to want to take a half-day at school on Friday," dad said with a slight laugh.

As I got up from the table, I said, "But you do know that I'm not a traitor for going up to Canada. I mean, this is my shot to play against the best. Maybe impress someone, you know....like it's my first step to making the NHL."

"Well," dad said in that father knows best voice of his. "The NHL is a long ways away, it's great to dream about it, but take a few steps back. It's a tremendous honor to be asked to play for the Red Raiders and what you want to take out of this is that you get to play with and against some great players. You'll gain a lot of experience and hopefully make some great friends. I just want you to enjoy yourself and… and it's great that we get to spend a lot of time together."

"Yeah, you're right. Thanks for the pep talk," I said looking down.

"You're welcome," he said.

That night Terry came over to watch the Penguins and Rangers game and we had a great time. Actually, I'm not sure which of us had more fun, me, Terry or my dad. Yes, my dad watched with us. Before the game started he asked if he could watch. What could I say? "No dad, you can't watch… that is all there is to it." You know how it is when an adult sits with a few kids and watches a television show or a sporting event. Everyone ends up feeling uncomfortable but in our case watching the Pens and Rangers game was a lot of fun.

Terry could go very easily from talking about the left wing lock and the trap to how he liked to read the poetry of John Donne and George Herbert who were two British 16th century poets (I only found out who they were by asking him.) He would tell you in excruciating detail why Wayne Gretzky was the best hockey player, although I disagreed saying that Mario Lemieux was better than the Great One, and in the next breath tell you that Bob Dylan's best album was "Blood on the Tracks"; my dad disagreed saying "Blonde on Blonde" was his best.

That debate sent them off on a tangent about Bruce Springsteen and Pete Townshend and who was the better songwriter. This led to my dad breaking out pictures of when he dressed up as Bruce Springsteen and my mom dressed up as Madonna for a Halloween party they went to.

Terry told us that his parents were both professors at Carnegie Mellon University which explained a lot about his knowledge of two 16th century British poets and that he had two older brothers who were in college and they also played hockey. He mentioned how his brother Ben was the star of their high school team that won the state championship when he was senior. He was the captain of the team and he led the league in goals with 45 in only 20 games. That same year his other older brother, Alan, was the starting goaltender and he had six shutouts that state championship season.

"When I was eight my parents made both of them keep a B average and they each had to go to the Carnegie Museum every week," he said.

"Why'd they have to go to the museum every week?" my dad asked.

"My parents thought that if they spent some time learning about Art and History that it would complement their school studies and they would become well-rounded kids," he said. "The ironic thing was that they enjoyed going to the museum so much that they both volunteer down there. My parents enjoyed going to their hockey games so much that they ended up buying season tickets to the Penguins games!"

"Your parents sound like they are pretty cool," I said.

"Different," Terry said with a smile.

"Well, what about me," my dad said. "I'm pretty cool. No, make that very cool!"

"In your own way, I guess," I said as I rolled my eyes.

"Well, at least I have a cool son," dad said.

"Who will one day be in the NHL," I replied back.

"Tom," dad said slowly breaking the light and happy mood, "let's just take it slow. One tournament at a time and even one game at a time."

"Oh, I will make it," I said matter-of-factly. "The tournaments will help a college or pro scout see me and I'll be on their radar."

"It's true, Mr. Leonard," Terry said chiming in. "He's that good and I can see him playing in the NHL."

"Well, Terry," dad said quietly. "You're a smart kid, you know a lot about Springsteen and Dylan. You also know hockey better then most adults. However, at least for now, you are not working in scouting or personnel for an NHL team and I think we all have to ease back on the NHL talk."

"Sure, Mr. Leonard," Terry said.

"Oh, yeah, um, right Captain Killjoy," I said and then after a second I couldn't hold back the laugh that I had been trying to stifle. Terry took my lead and started to laugh and even my dad joined in the laughter.

I didn't ask Terry about the Magic Rats and what happened with them not making the playoffs. He didn't bring it up either which was good. He did ask a lot about the Red Raiders and what we did in practices and in the tournament games. It was nice to be able to talk to him about what happened there and not have him mad or jealous that I missed the Magic Rats games. I didn't think that the other guys on the team, well, most of them at least, were interested in how I did in Canada and I really couldn't blame them.

We got the call later in the week that there would be a one hour practice on Friday night and then our first tournament game was set for 9:30 a.m. on Saturday. We had a second game set for 5:30 p.m. and then we'd play on Sunday as well. We were guaranteed three games and there were only eight teams in the tournament so if we won our two games on Saturday we would be playing for the tournament championship on Sunday. If not, we would be in one of the consolation games. I knew how much this tournament meant to Coach Gilmour. That he scheduled a practice the night before the tournament was a strong message to the team.

I got out of school early and we got on the PA turnpike headed for Oakville, Ontario which was about a five hour drive for us. We got into Oakville, ate and then headed over to the rink where the practice was going to take place. The practice started at 8:00 p.m. which, coincidently, was the time we made it to the rink since we had gotten lost.

Man, was it frustrating as we drove around and around Oakville looking for the Kinoak Arena on Warminster Drive. My dad even stopped and asked people on the street for directions. He wasn't too fond of *EVER* asking anyone for directions. Even so, it did help as a nice lady gave us a detailed set of right and left turns and we finally found the rink.

I ran in and the guys were already on the ice. My dad came in quickly behind me and motioned for Coach Gilmour to come over. I started walking very quickly toward the dressing rooms and I heard dad explaining to the coach that we got lost. I got my equipment on as quickly as I could and as soon as I hit the ice I heard the coach's whistle blow.

"Tommy, your dad explained what happened," he yelled across the ice as all of the guys looked over at me. "I understand you're traveling a good ways up here and you're not familiar with the area. The bottom line is that you were late and as punishment give me twenty five push ups and five laps around the rink. Now let's go!"

That was probably the nicest thing he said to me during the practice. No excuses, I played really bad. I couldn't hit the net with my shots and I was out of position constantly on defense which drove Coach Gilmour nuts. It was just like what Garth had told me before…the Coach always wanted us in our position and he wasn't too cool with defensemen rushing the puck. So, guess what I did, twice? I tried rushing the puck in our scrimmage and both times I got caught up ice and both times Landon ended up putting the puck in the net. After each goal, Coach Gilmour yelled, "Tommy, what in the world is going on with you?"

It wasn't pretty that night and, believe it or not, that was the highlight of my weekend as I was on the ice for six goals in the first Saturday game and two more in the evening game and we lost both games. I was very tentative and didn't play with a lot of confidence and our goalies, Dennis and Jarrett, couldn't stop a beach ball in either of those games. We came back on Sunday morning and beat a team from Deerhurst, Ontario.

"Tommy, Coach Gilmour would like to talk to you and your dad, okay," Coach Clemmons said to me in the locker room as I was zipping up my equipment bag after the Deerhurst game.

"Me *and* my dad?" I asked.

"Yes, both of you," he said quickly. "I'll find your dad and send him back"

"Sure," I said slowly.

Landon and Noah had heard Coach Clemmons and they, at first, looked away from me and then looked at me and just shrugged their shoulders as if they were saying, "I don't know what he wants to talk to you about but whatever it is, it can't be good."

"Coach Gilmour, um Coach Clemmons said you wanted to see me and my dad," I said nervously.

"Yeah, Tommy, let's step out of the room for a second and talk in the hall," he said.

"Um, is something the matter?" I asked.

"No, uh, well, let's just walk out into the hall and we can talk out there," he said looking straight ahead.

We walked into the hallway right outside of the dressing room and no one was around. The teams that were playing in the championship game were already on the ice. Coach Clemmons brought my dad to where Coach Gilmour and I were standing in the hallway and he looked like he was a little surprised to be asked to have an impromptu meeting with the coach and me.

"Thanks Colin," Coach Gilmour said to Coach Clemmons who turned around and walked away. "Gentlemen, you've only known me a short time but you know that I don't mince my words. Tommy, the reason I wanted to talk to you and your dad is that I have to pass along some bad news to you. We're going to cut you from the team. You won't be playing with us in the Ottawa tournament."

"But, uh, Coach Gilmour, um…why?" I asked.

"Tommy…you're a good player and one day you have the chance to be a great player. But at this point in time you're not at the AAA level. You have a lot of talent, but you have to work on the positional part of the game. Your skating is good and you have a good shot but your puck handling needs some work and you have a lot to learn about playing defense and working with the four other guys on the ice. My guess is that on your hometown team you rush the puck a lot. Right?" he asked.

"Sure, I mean I like to rush the puck and—"

"You like to shoot the puck off the rush or maybe try to go coast-to-coast, right?"

"Well, yeah, but—"

"You saw him, Coach Gilmour, when he won the Etobicoke tournament MVP. Part of the reason he won that is because his game is to find the gaps and go coast-to-coast like you said," dad chimed in.

"I understand that, Mr. Leonard," Coach Gilmour said in a serious tone as he turned toward dad. "Up here in AAA he's playing against kids, talent-wise, who are at a minimum his equal if not more highly-skilled. We have to go with the players we think we can win with and right now, I'm sorry to say Tommy, you're simply not ready to play at this level."

"So, it's just a matter of experience?" dad asked Coach Gilmour.

"Maybe, maybe not. I can't tell you now," Coach Gilmour said. "It's possible if he goes home and works on his game, becomes more of a team-oriented and defensive-minded player, yeah sure he can come back next year and try out."

"Try out?" both me and my dad said at the same time. "He didn't have to try out this time around," dad said.

"Look, guys, I'm just being straight with you," Coach Gilmour said as he looked at me first and then dad. "Tommy, you are a very talented kid, I just can't predict how you're going to progress. I've seen kids without your skating ability make the jump from AA to AAA and I've had other kids who were as talented as you but they never made their mark because they didn't know, or want to know, how to *play* the position. You have a bright future, but you have some work to do. If you learn the game, learn the position and make the players around you *better*…then Tommy you'll have a spot on my team anytime."

He held his hand out and I shook it and then my dad shook it. Coach Gilmour then said, "I'll be in touch with you throughout the year, I'll check up on you and hopefully next year things will work out for you up here. This kind of thing happens. We had three kids last year who played in a few tournaments that we had to let go. Look, I have to run, but keep your head up and do what I said and I'm sure we'll see you here next year."

The coach headed over to the stands and dad and I just stood there motionless. He was looking down at the ground and I was just looking straight ahead, neither of us knew what to say. About a minute passed when I finally said to him, "Let me grab my stuff and I'll be out." He just nodded okay and I walked back to the locker room, hoping all of the guys had left already.

Turns out Phillip and Pierre Davidoff were still in the locker room. They were wrestling over a can of Mountain Dew and I don't know if they even noticed me come into the room. They stopped wrestling each other for a second and when I said, "Later boys" to them they each nodded and then started wrestling each other again. As I looked back, all I could see was hair flying and a can of Mountain Dew rolling on the ground. This would serve as my final memory of Red Raider hockey.

Chapter 11
Regarding
(my departure and my so-called NHL dream, Part 2)

"So…" my dad said as we drove on the QEW headed home. We had been on the road for about an hour and I had not said one word since getting in the car. Dad had tried a few times to engage in some conversation but I couldn't even look at him. I was just staring out the window.

"Well…it was a good experience…you know, it was fun," he mumbled. "Tom, are you going to be silent the whole way home?"

"What do you want me to say, dad?" I snapped. "That I'm disappointed? That I'm very sad? That I feel stupid? Well, then, yes to all of the above…I simply don't know how a few bad games and one practice can get someone dropped. How is that even possible? It's not fair."

"Life's not fair, Tom." he said sternly. "Look, if getting cut by the Red Raiders is the worst thing that happens to you, then you should consider yourself pretty lucky. You know there are kids starving all around the world, kids living on the streets—"

"Please don't give me the 'kids starving in Africa' story," I said as I quickly turned towards him. "I know that one already and this isn't tragic by any means but still... I couldn't cut the mustard up here with these guys and the other guys on the Magic Rats will know I messed up," I said.

"Yeah and so what," dad said. "You did your best and you were asked to play up here. You have to be a pretty special player just to be asked to play in these tournaments. You have nothing to be ashamed of!"

"Sounds good, dad," I said sharply. "Now, go tell Billy Horton that I played in two tournaments and that I was asked to leave. See how fast he starts laughing, go tell Coach Brantford and see how fast he says 'I told you so.' Oh, I give that about ten seconds."

"Doesn't matter," dad said convincingly.

He started staring at me as a red pickup truck drove by us going about ninety miles an hour.

"What are you trying to say?" I asked.

"It doesn't matter what anyone thinks. All that matters is what you think about yourself. This isn't the end, you just have to listen to what Coach Gilmour said and work on some parts of your game and you'll be right back up here next year."

"There's not going to be a next year," I said sadly.

"What do you mean, there's not going to be a next year?" dad asked.

"I don't know if I want to play next year," I said, my voice trailing off at the end.

"Why, Tom? You heard what the coach said. You know, last week you were dreaming of going to the NHL and now you don't even want to play with your friends back home? It's just a minor setback Tom, you have all the talent—" dad said before I cut in.

"You keep talking about my talent and my dream. Don't you realize the dream just died in Oakville and this talent you keep talking about wasn't able to keep me on the team. I have just enough talent to be considered not worthy of being on an elite team," I said loudly.

"So, let me get this straight. You're done with hockey, you're going to quit playing?" dad asked me and then he started to chuckle.

"Yup, I'm done."

"So, you're quitting?"

"Quitting, giving it up, whatever you want to call it. I'm done playing."

"Wow, retired at age thirteen. That must be a record of some kind!"

"You got it buddy, finished, done."

"Your Granddad would find this all very amusing. You know how proud he was of you. Right now if he was here, he'd tell you how disappointed he would be in you for quitting or giving up hockey after one minor setback."

"Please leave Grandpa out of this," I said firmly.

"He would have loved to watch you play. But just as importantly, he would have loved just being with you… talking to you. And he would be the first to tell you that you are making a mistake," dad said. "He always taught me never to give in or give up. 'Keep fighting, never stop' he'd tell me when things didn't go my way. Believe me, growing up, they hardly ever went my way. But I kept on working hard."

"I don't know, dad," I said quietly looking again out the window. "Let me give it some thought. Fall's still a long ways away and I have to think this one through."

"Tom," he said in a soothing tone, "believe me, you are capable of greatness in all that you do. You just have to work as hard as you possibly can. Remember when you were playing Dek Hockey a few years ago and your Granddad said, 'Give me what you got and then give me some more.' You remember that don't you?"

"Yeah," I said as I nodded my head up and down all the while looking out the window.

"So, that's what you have to do. Listen to what Coach Gilmour said. Work on the being more of a team player and play better positional hockey. When you play with the Magic Rats—"

"I didn't say that I was going to play for the Magic Rats."

"Pardon me…*If* you play for the Magic Rats then make sure you listen to Coach Brantford and do what he says. Even if you think he's wrong or if you disagree with his methods. When all is said and done, someday…you will get there. One day you will fly."

"I'll fly?"

"It's an old expression that—"

"It's an old expression that Granddad used to say," we said in unison and then started to laugh.

My dad had a tendency to talk about my Granddad. Even though he passed away four years ago, he'd always say how he was thinking of him and then there were the numerous sayings, stories, jokes, and advice that Granddad gave him. I think about him a lot, too. He always understood me better than anyone else, my dad included.

After the events of today I *really, really* wish Granddad was here to tell me that everything would be okay and that one day I *would* fly.

Chapter 12
Remarkable

I was able to keep my less-than-remarkable news about being cut from the guys on the Magic Rats because most of them went to different schools in our district, although Billy, Frankie and the Bobby's were in my school and in the same grade as me. Frankie and I would hang out at lunch time. He had told me about not making the playoffs but he was pretty tight-lipped about what was said in the aftermath. He told me he was going to play in a summer three-on-three league and asked me if I wanted to play. After he said that, he added, only if I wasn't playing those weekends with what he called "the Canada team." We were friends so I finally broke down and told him on the last day of school that I wouldn't be playing in Canada because I was cut from the team.

For an uncomfortable few seconds he just started at me as if the words I had spoken were not in English. Then he looked at me with a big look of pity and said he sorry and asked what happened. I told him it was too long a story and I left it at that. I asked him to keep it to himself, secure in the knowledge that he would blab the news to one of the Bobby's and then the whole school would know that I got cut. I purposely told him on the last day just so that I could get the news out but not have to explain myself a million times to everyone who was wondering why I got cut.

We had a half day on the last day of school and then two days later was our district-wide Kennywood Day. Kennywood Park is this wonderful amusement park in West Mifflin, PA. Even though I wasn't really into the rides, I loved to go once or twice a summer and play the games and eat the fries there. I had made plans with Terry to hang out as he was also a non-rider. Even though he and I had talked a lot, I didn't tell him I got cut from the Red Raiders. I wanted to tell him in person and Kennywood seemed like the best place to do it as I didn't want him to dwell on it or ask a million questions about what happened.

One of the tamer rides at Kennywood is the Turnpike and there was a small line waiting to get in the little motorized cars and "drive" around. I figured that now was as good a time as any, while we were waiting in line, to tell Terry about what had happened in Canada.

"I wanted to tell you something," I said as we stood in line.

"What is it? Oh, I know, you want to drive the blue car, number 29 right?" he said with a smile.

"No, man…it's some bad news about Canada. I got cut," I said not making eye contact with him.

"Cut! I thought you were doing so good," he said incredulously.

"I just wasn't good *enough*," I said choosing my words carefully. "The guys up there were at a whole other level than I was and I had a bad practice and then I screwed up royally in the Oakville tournament. The coach up there basically told me not to come back for the Ottawa tournament."

"You messed up?"

"Yeah, I played bad," I said as we moved up a few steps in the line. "The coach was really big on playing good positional hockey and he was really strict about playing a team game."

"You're a team guy. You're the best player, the best defenseman for rushing the puck," Terry said throwing up his arms.

"He didn't want me to rush the puck," I said quickly. "Plus there were forwards up there that I couldn't keep up with. Guys on my own team were getting past me."

"I'm real sorry, man. Maybe they'll call you back at some point this summer, you know with vacations and stuff," said Terry.

"I seriously doubt it," I said. "The coach said if I improved on the team aspect of my game and get better defensively then maybe next year I can try out for the team."

"Try out? You didn't have to try out this year."

"Man, that is what me and my dad said to the coach. But it's his team, his rules I guess. Plus, he'd probably want to see in practice if I could keep up with his guys. Still, in the end, it's all a moot point," I said.

"What do you mean, it's a moot point?" he asked.

"It doesn't matter, I'm done playing. In Canada and here…I'm through with hockey," I said.

"You are joking, right?" Terry said as he quickly stopped in his tracks. A lady who was behind him bumped into him when he pulled up. "You're still going to play for the Magic Rats, right?"

"Nah, I'm done with hockey for now, man. I just don't feel like playing it right now and who knows, maybe I'll never play again," I said.

"You simply cannot be serious," he said.

"Why is it so hard for you to believe me?" I asked.

"You're an awesome player, and you want to play in the NHL someday. Didn't you tell me before that that was your dream?" Terry asked.

"Like I told my dad, that dream died in Oakville. It's over, done, finished." I said as we moved up to the front of the line. We would be the next twosome to get in the cars.

"You're wasting your talent, man," Terry said in a pleading tone. "You're too good a hockey player and too talented a hockey player to let all that slip away."

"You and my dad are on the same wavelength, because on the ride back home he started talking in that father-knows-all-and-is-wise-mode about my talent. I explained to him and I'll explain to you that this so-called great talent I possess wasn't good enough to get me very far. If I can't make it up in Canada I don't know if I want to play anymore. I just don't know," I said as we got into white car number 45.

"I don't need a full summer of you trying to convince me to play. The guys on the team are already steamed at me for not playing in the last three games and when they find out that I got cut by the Canada team, well, some of them will be happy and think that I got what I deserved for abandoning them," I added.

"Maybe. I know there are probably some guys still upset with you. There are more who would welcome you back to the team. They're your friends and the guys who were upset with you would probably come around when they realized that having you gives us the best chance to win," Terry added as we went around the first corner of the Turnpike ride.

"Billy?" I said.

"Would he be happy to have you back?" Terry replied back to me.

"Yeah."

"No."

"See what I mean."

"That's just him."

"He's the captain and a bunch of guys follow his lead."

"Maybe," Terry said as we went up a small hill. "Who cares about how he feels, you know. You've got to do what is best for you but I really think playing with us would be your best move."

"Nah, I'm just fed up with the game," I said.

"How can you say that?" he asked loudly as the noise from the park threatened to drown out our voices. "I mean hockey is the greatest game on the planet and you play it really well. I can't imagine not playing or watching hockey, or playing a hockey video game or not reading about hockey in The Hockey News or Sports Illustrated—"

"I get your point, Terry," I said before he really got off and running on.

"I mean, you've done stuff in games that I can see myself doing…and then I wake up," he said and then laughed. "But, really, if you never play again, you've accomplished so much. The goals, the assists, the breakaway goals…it's just that…I," Terry said slowly.

"What…" I said.

"It's just that if you don't play anymore that you'll have done things that I'll never be able to do and the worst part is I really, really would be able to die a happy person if I simply scored one goal sometime. It doesn't have to be a pretty goal or a game-winning goal...just one stinking goal," Terry said as his voiced trailed off.

"You'll score a goal, don't worry," I insisted.

"Don't you see," he said as we went around another corner, the real cars from out on Kennywood Boulevard zipping past us. "You have this great gift, a great talent for playing hockey and if you quit you'll never know how far you can go with it. Maybe you don't play in college or in the NHL, but if you quit now you'll never know. I can practice and skate and skate and skate but I'll never be a great hockey player because I don't have *it*, what you and Stevie and a few other guys have. Maybe someday if I worked hard enough I could skate halfway decently and shoot hard and straight enough. To do the things in a game that you can do, those can't be taught or learned they come from inside you. Your heart, your desire...if you quit..."

"Then what?" I asked him.

"Then part of you, inside, will die," Terry said as we rode around the final turn. "Because I know how much you love hockey and if you don't play then 20 or 30 years from now you'll be wondering what if. What if you did keep playing, what if you were able to take it to the next level and the level after that. You quit now, you'll never know."

"Maybe, maybe you're right," I said as we stepped out of the car.

"I'm a hockey player for life," Terry said with a huge grin. "I'll be playing in those old guy leagues or coaching or doing something with hockey for as long as I live. Heck, I might even be buried with my skates on!"

"Well, I have a lot of time to think about it, but I appreciate your advice," I said.

"Anytime, anytime," Terry said as he patted me on the back.

Chapter 13
Redemption
(Part 1)

The fall had always been my favorite time of the year. I hated the heat of the summer and even though I really despised the term "back to school", I loved the September and October time frame. The leaves start falling and the cool air makes it a great time of year. Terry and my dad knew how I felt but neither gave me the business or questioned me at any point over the summer about playing for the Magic Rats.

When it came time to decide, I was still unsure of what to do. The pep talks I had gotten from my dad and Terry were helpful but I was still upset about what went down in Canada along with being called a traitor by Coach Brantford. I felt like I wasn't part of either team.

I'll always remember the date, September 10th, that I had to make my decision as the enrollment form had to be turned into the league president. It was my dad's birthday and we were going to have a surprise party for him. The gift I got him, once again, was Old Spice cologne from the Thrift Drugstore which was in the shopping plaza that was around the corner from our house. He always smiled and looked appreciative but after the third time, spanning one birthday and two Hanukkah's, I think the thrill of getting a bottle of Old Spice cologne probably wore off.

I thought that if I gave him the Old Spice *and* told him that I was going to play for the Magic Rats that that would make him happy and I really did want to make him happy, especially on his birthday.

As I was looking at the enrollment form, twisting it around and around as I sat on my bed, I kept thinking back to how I felt on that ride home from Oakville after being cut. To me, it wasn't fair or just and if given the chance, a proper chance I could play with those guys. If I could have played my game, my style…if Coach Gilmour *would* have let me or given me free rein to play my style I would have shown him what I could do! If only I would have been able to tell him, or show him that I was *right*!

I knew the game, regardless of what Coach Gilmour said, I knew how to play positional hockey and I always was a team guy, an unselfish player. I shook my head and pounded my fist on the bed, I will show Coach Gilmour, I'll prove him wrong, I thought. I grabbed a pen from my desk and signed my name and dated the form. Redemption, I whispered to myself, redemption would be mine!

Chapter 14
Rebuild & Reconstruct

Sunday, October 1st, the first night of practice for the Magic Rats and right after dinner, I was ready to leave even though practice didn't start for two more hours. I had come full circle in that I didn't want anything to do with hockey, to now having to prove myself and gain back the respect of my teammates.When I told my dad that I was going to play for the Magic Rats back on his birthday, he was kind of low-key about it. "That's good, Tom," was about all he offered up. Terry was the same way when I called him with the news. He said he knew all along that I would be back so it wasn't much of a surprise.

As we got close to Fairview, dad said nothing at all. I wasn't sure if he was waiting for me to start yakking or what so I finally said to him, "Penny for your thoughts."

"Oh, I don't know," he murmured. "Nice night, maybe I'll hang around a bit and sneak into practice...see how you're doing."

"I think I'll be fine," I offered back. "Hey this is the new me, I'm a new man. I'm goin' in with the idea of playing good positional defense, I'm going to do my best to spread the puck around and be a good teammate. In some people's eyes around the locker room, maybe they're thinking that I let them down last season so I'm going to work at 150 percent to earn their trust and respect back."

"Well, Tom," dad said proudly, "you've really thought this through and you have a good attitude. Follow the Coaches' instructions…seriously, listen to them—"

"I will, I will," I said as I shifted around in the seat.

"I just want you to have learned from what happened up in Canada," he said as we pulled into Fairview's parking lot. "Use what happened up there as a learning experience because you can't change it."

Dad parked the car and put it in park. "So, are you ready to go?"

Quickly, I replied, "Yeah, definitely. Are you going to come in and watch?"

He let out a short laugh and said, "Well, maybe I'll sneak in a little later." Becoming serious he then said, "I want you to enjoy yourself. Remember what your Granddad used to say 'they call it *playing* for a reason.' It's supposed to be fun."

"Thanks, dad," I said quietly.

"Okay, buddy," he said as he patted me on the right shoulder. "I'll catch you later."

With that, I got my gear out of the back and made the long walk up the wooden, creaky stairs and walked into the rink. It was just like it always was, freezing cold. Then there was the hockey locker room smell, and anyone who has ever been in a hockey locker room knows *that* smell, which was very thick in the air. Right before I walked in I just kept thinking about how I was about to experience a moment that I had been playing through in mind and visualizing how it would go for months. The thought of should I just walk in and find a seat or say hello to each guy or maybe even just yell out, "I'm back!" I just wasn't sure what to do or say.

I pushed the door open and walked inside and even though I had run this whole moment through my head a thousand times, I just kept thinking that I had the words loser, failure, wash out and traitor scrawled on my face. I was standing in the room and most of the guys were already there and getting their equipment on.

A few of them looked up as I stood there but didn't say anything. Bobby R. nodded and said, "Hey Tom." Terry who was in the back left hand corner waved for me to come back. That was it, no "Hey Tom, I hear you got cut" or "Tom, what are you doing here playing with us lowlifes." Nope, it was a blissfully uneventful moment which I had played up to be something that it wasn't. Stupid me.

A little later the third and fourth line guys like Reese, Larry and Eric each gave me big slaps on the back and said good to see you which was nice since I didn't go to school with them and thus it was the first time I had seen them since the spring. Even Steve, who barely said boo to me, walked over to where Terry and I were sitting and he offered me a handshake and said welcome back.

Maybe they weren't that mad at me or maybe they realized that we were a better team with me than without me. Regardless, it was a lot of fun to be in the room with those guys. Bobby H. would talk about his older brother who was always getting in trouble for something, Frankie usually had a story about a girl he was chasing and then there was Terry who never stopped talking. Tonight he was regaling me with a story about how he and his dad were debating if Wayne Gretzky would be as great as he is if he was born in the USA instead of in Canada. Terry argued that he'd still be a great hockey player while his dad reasoned that if he had lived in Oklahoma or Arizona he would have grown up to be a great baseball player.

Like everything else in life, all good times must come to an end, and the end of the good time I was having at practice came when Coach Brantford walked into the room. It was as if the Darth Vader music was playing behind him as he came in, with his skates on, and asked for everyone to quiet down.

"Okay, guys, first practice of the year. It's always a fun one, right?" he said as a few guys laughed. "Lots of skating; we may not even use a puck, we'll see."

There were a few groans with that announcement but no one should have been surprised about that because at last year's first practice we skated for two straight hours.

"I did want to make a quick announcement," he said as he looked over at me. "We have a few new players, Ian and Chris, who are around here somewhere. We also have one guy returning. You may have heard what happened in Canada, but never the less he's back for, hopefully, the *entire* season. So, Tom, let's hope we have you here with us, giving us your full support each game and practice."

I just nodded my head and looked around at the staring faces. I didn't know whether to feel good that I was wanted or feel really bad because of that little public flogging that I just took. I took a deep breath and thought that the coach just threw me under the bus because the team didn't make the playoffs last year and I was a convenient target since I wasn't there when it happened. Fine, now I hoped he would just move onto the actual practice.

"Coach Malone and I have devised the lines and defensive pairings and we put them on the chalkboard outside of the room here. So, see where you are. After warm-up, first and second line and defense line up behind me and the third and fourth lines and defense line up behind Coach Malone. Let's Go!"

The team filed out of the locker room in a single file line and each guy stopped and looked at the board for a quick second. When it was my turn I looked at the board, blinked my eyes and then squinted to make sure that I was seeing what I thought I saw: D4 – Tom and Terry.

I just assumed, which is always dangerous, that I'd be on the number one defensive pairing with David. Getting lost in the shuffle of playing my position better and being a better team player was the thought of *playing time*. It was going to be difficult to work on those parts of my game from the bench.

On the bright side, I thought as we all had our warm-up skate, maybe playing on the fourth defensive pairing was just a temporary thing. Hey, maybe it was just for this practice. Once the actual games start, I rationalized that I would be back in the number one pairing with David and Gregg would slide back to team up with Terry.

The other nice thing was being able to team up with Terry. I would be able to help him out by giving him some pointers on skating, passing and shooting and he could help me with the strategy part of the game. I had it all worked out.

So I thought. The lines and defensive pairings were inconsequential as for this Practice. Coach Brantford skated us almost through the ice and into the cement. Back and forth, up and around and back up and down the ice we went. Finally, with about 15 minutes to go he got the puck bag out, blew the whistle and shouted, "Lines and defense one and two and Michael, you guys head down with Coach Malone to the far end to scrimmage, everyone else stay here with me for a passing drill."

As if to add insult to injury we did a routine passing drill while the other guys had a scrimmage. I was so bored my attention, and eyes, drifted to the guys scrimmaging. This didn't sit very well with Coach Brantford who blew his whistle and then came skating over towards me in a hurry. He then got right in my face and yelled, "Wanna be with those guys, huh Tom?"

"Well, yeah, I mean…but I was just watching for a second. Sorry coach," I mumbled. All of the guys on my side of the ice stopped doing the drill and were looking at me and the coach.

"Then maybe you should have thought twice about running up to Canada and leaving everyone here out to dry. Did you think there weren't going to be any repercussions for you costing us a chance to make the playoffs," he hollered.

"I'm sorry, Coach," I whispered, my eyes looking down.

"Don't apologize to me, apologize to these guys," he said as he pointed his left handed stick in a circular motion."Apologize to each of them, apologize to Coach Malone, apologize to the fans that came to see us go against Colts Hill and get whacked. There's lots of apologizing to do Tom. Show me that you're in it this year to win it and maybe you'll get the chance to play with those guys down there instead of watching them during drills."

Coach Brantford blew his whistle and yelled for us to hit the showers and thus ended the longest minute of my life. It only felt like an hour, I would later tell Terry. He told me how he and a bunch of the other guys didn't think it was fair of the coach to do what he did and I told him I appreciated that. Still, the damage was done, I was completely humiliated in front of the team and basically told by the coach to apologize to each guy and then and only then could I try and work my way out of his doghouse and get back on the first defensive unit.

So, how do you make those who are uncomfortable around you feel even more uncomfortable…you walk up to them directly, look them in eye and say your piece. Which I did to each guy who was still in the room. I walked up to them, one-by-one, told them I was sorry about what happened at the end of last season and that they had my commitment to making this year a championship season. 20 times I did this, 18 times to the guys on the team and to both Coach Malone and Coach Brantford. Both of them looked a little embarrassed when I apologized. Even though I still felt picked on and singled out, I wasn't going to express that, I was simply going to do what the coach told me to do.

Chapter 15
Restraint

"Did you sneak in?" I asked my dad as we pulled out of the Fairview lot after practice.

"No, I had to stop at the grocery store. So, tell me what happened. How'd it go?" dad asked.

I paused for a second and then said, "Well, if you take away the last few minutes when Coach Brantford laid into me in front of the whole team about going to Canada and letting them down. Heck, other than that little bit of fun and merriment, the practice was great. Oh, and then there was the whole bit about having to apologize to each guy on the team and being demoted to the fourth defensive pairing with Terry."

Dad let out a little chuckle and then said, "I don't agree with the verbal beat down in front of the team, but I'm sure he had his reasons for doing it." We came up to a red light and after stopping he turned to me and said, "As far as playing on the fourth defensive unit, on that one I'm sure he's trying to motivate you, not punish you."

"If you would have seen or heard him yelling at me, you'd change your tune, dad. He's mad at me for leaving the team to play in Canada and now he's taking it out on me with the yelling and playing with the third and fourth unit guys. That's it, I mean it's just a punishment and how long it will last, only he knows."

"Look, Tom," he said as he faced forward as the red light changed to green. As he gripped the steering wheel tightly he said, "You have to show the coach and the guys on the team that you can take it and even come back for more. Trust me, his dad was the same way with a kid on our team named Maxwell Bamberg. He was our best right wing and Coach Brantford senior used to think that if he got a hat trick in a game, that he could have had two hat tricks if he was playing to his full ability. He just rode him harder than anyone else on the team to try and motivate him to be his absolute best."

"Do you think that was the right thing for the coach to ride him like he did?" I asked.

"No," he shot back. "But, the coach's intentions were good. He wanted Max to realize his potential. The beauty of Coach Brantford senior was that he was great at knowing when to kick a guy in his butt and he could just as easily pat a guy on the back if he felt he needed it. I want you to be strong enough to withstand your Coach Brantford's yelling. If he didn't think you were capable of taking it, he wouldn't dish it out. For example, does he scream or holler at Terry?"

"No, never really," I said.

"That's because he knows Terry will never be much better than he already is, no knock against him. He knows what you can do and the best way you can beat him is to take it and say, 'Thank you sir, may I have another.' You gotta believe me, Tom."

"Alright," I said and then let out a big sigh. "I trust your judgment, I just hope you're right."

My dad, and my mom for that matter, I learned as I grew up were always right about stuff. Not just about wearing a coat when it was cold or putting sun block on when it was sunny, no, they were right about how situations with people would eventually work out. They were like the Harlem Globetrotters, 15,000 wins and zero losses.

Dad was spot on right about the verbal "motivation" from Coach Brantford. During the second practice of the season he rode me hard about almost everything. My skating stride, the way I was leaning into a skate stop and not having two hands on the stick at all times were just a few of the mistakes I heard, loud and clear, that I was making. I scrimmaged with the fourth line against the third line and I resisted each opportunity I had to grab the puck and go around and through those guys. I could have done it easily enough but instead I passed the puck off to one of the forwards or over to Terry.

At the end of that second practice the coach had me scoop up all of the pucks and put them in the puck bags while all of the other guys on the team got off the ice. I know Billy was getting a good laugh about that. I did get the last laugh as after I gathered up all of the pucks I asked the coach if there was anything else I could do. He gave me a mean look, then turned away from me and mumbled no. Just like dad said, "Thank you sir, may I have another."

I talked to Terry just about every night on the phone; he had now become my best friend. About 95 percent of the conversations we had revolved around the Magic Rats. He seemed to walk on eggshells occasionally when I'd talk about the way Coach Brantford was treating me. I was talking to him on the phone before our third practice and I kept insisting to him that the treatment I got in the first two practices wasn't bothering me. I said, "I'm going to be the bigger man and my hard work is going to pay off. I know I'm earning the Coach's respect and the team's respect back."

"Tom, the guys already respect you," he said. "At this point it's just uncomfortable and kind of ridiculous. You apologized to the guys, I mean, what else can you do?"

"Whatever he says, man. I have to pass each of his tests and then hopefully I can get back in the saddle, you know," I said as I looked out my bedroom window at the monsoon-like conditions outside. The rain was teeming off the roof and lightning was filling up the early evening sky. "My dad says it's just a test and if I can hang in there I'll be okay. He said that Coach Brantford's old man used to do that kind of thing all of the time."

"I know you told me that your dad is always right about things, but what if he's got this one messed up? It's like, it's possible that he's wrong and the coach is just going to mess with you and the guys will lose respect for you if you keep taking it."

"So what should I do? Tell him to leave me alone or quit?" I asked.

"I don't know that answer," Terry said. There was silence on the line for about 15 seconds until he continued, "I just don't want to see you get picked on, buddy. I really don't want you to quit. I just wish the coach would wise up and set the team straight with you in the first unit so we can win some games."

"Me too, Terry, me too," I said slowly. I told him I had to get ready for practice and that I'd see him in a little while.

Now my brain was really messed up. What if I had gone about this whole thing wrong? What if my dad was wrong about the coach and maybe the team in general in that they were feeling sorry for me. What if, indeed, the guys thought I was some kind of goof or a loser for taking the abuse the coach was dishing out? I always felt I was well respected and liked. But what if they were viewing me in a harsh light or thinking that I wasn't the player I used to be since I got cut from the Canadian team and now the coach was treating me like a dog? I couldn't come up with any answers in the short term, on my own, I figured I'd just get my dad's take and make sure I was doing the right thing.

Can I ask you something, dad?" I said as we were about halfway to Fairview. Practice number three was to start in about a half hour.

"Sure, what is it?" he asked.

"What if I am doing the wrong thing. You know, in the way I am handling things with Coach Brantford. The way he's been so tough on me and the whole 'yes sir, can I have another' thing. What if the guys see me taking a lot of guff and they think that I am now a lesser player?" I asked.

He pursed his lips, squinted and then said, "All you can control in this world, is your own attitude and your own actions. You can't control how the coach is going to treat or act towards you or how other people interpret those actions. Do I believe that you'll be better off by taking what the coach is dishing out? I do. I believe in the end that the guys on the team will have a greater respect for you since they'll see that you could have quit and that instead you hung in there and were able to rise above it. Look at it this way, you've had two practices, you haven't even started the games yet. It's two minutes into the start of the game, you still have almost three full periods to go. Just stick with it."

"What if you're wrong?" I asked him. "Seriously, what if you are wrong? There is that possibility, you know."

He laughed and then said, "Tom, it's not whether I'm right or wrong. I'm telling you, based on my life experience, what I *believe* to be the right course of action to take. I've gone through similar things like what you are going through now and I wish I knew back then what I know now. I'm trying to help you out."

"Yeah, but maybe times change and people change," I said loudly as I was becoming more agitated. "Maybe I should have just chucked it in this year. I'm playin' with the fourth liners, I'm picking up the pucks after practice and I'm supposed to smile and thank the coach for pointing out if I'm breathing wrong."

"Great!" he said as he slammed his fist onto the steering wheel. "Quit the team, that will solve everything. Why go out there and work hard, do the right thing if you'll only get to play with the fourth line guys. That is perfect justification to quit and never play again!"

"What do you mean? What are you *talking* about?" I asked.

"What I'm *talking* about is that playing, playing in and of itself is just one part of the equation. You play the game for exercise, to have fun and be with your friends. What makes playing hockey so great is that through the game you learn about teamwork, hard work and what it means to be on a team. Whether you play with the first, second, third or fourth liners is inconsequential. Hockey has always and will always be about the team," he said.

"That all sounds good, dad," I said as the windshield wipers made that super squeaky sound that they make when they are going full-tilt. "Although, this is unlike anything I've ever gone through."

"All the more reason to not quit, to hang in there and look back someday and realize what a huge mountain you had to climb up. If you can climb it, you'll realize that you can do anything you set your mind to. You can't just quit every time you don't get your way, Tom," he said as his voice, which started out soft, got louder. "I did not, and will not, raise a quitter or someone who folds up the tent when things aren't going right or his way."

"Well, you don't know what I'm going through inside," I said in full attack mode. "You never played at the level I've played at and you don't know what it feels like to have that taken away from you. I've lost it all, my shot at a scholarship, getting drafted, playing in the NHL. It's all gone now and now I can't even crack the lineup. My dreams, they're done and all you're telling me is to 'learn from the experience.' Well, I don't wanna learn from this experience, okay, dad. All I ever wanted to do was play hockey and now that's disappearing. What am I going to do now?'

"You're thirteen, Tom! You have your whole life in front of you. You can do anything you want," he said as we pulled into Fairview's lot. We bounced up and down as we drove over the numerous potholes, the water splashing everywhere as we moved forward. "You can be a doctor, an architect, a window washer, whatever you want to do or become will happen if you put your mind to it and work hard enough."

"Well I don't want to be like you working in an office or like Granddad driving around selling stuff. I know that," I yelled.

"You don't mean that," he said with a shocked look on his face. "Your Granddad was loved by all of his customers. They'd tell me what a special guy he was. Don't diminish what he did."

As the car came to a stop I said, "I just want to get inside."

"I'm not sure if I'm going to come in and watch," he said quietly.

I got out of the car, opened the back door, got my gear and then said, "Don't come in, you won't like what you see anyway. Better yet, have mom come and pick me up." I then slammed the back door, walked toward the front entrance and didn't look back.

As I sloshed my way up Fairview's wooden steps, I finally looked back and saw my dad's car pull away. I took a deep breath and then walked in. The whole argument had happened so fast. I felt bad about what I said, I didn't meant what I said about not wanting to be like my dad and Granddad. It was just said in the heat of the moment and it was the anger and frustration I was feeling over the one-two punch of getting cut by the Red Raiders and now not playing for the Magic Rats.

Sitting next to Terry and talking with him temporarily took my mind off the argument I had just had with my dad. On the walk out to the rink I thought about the argument for a few seconds, my conscience was working triple-time, and now I felt really, really bad about what I said to him. Maybe I should have called the house before the practice started and apologized, but now it was too late.

Once practice started, the argument did get pushed to the back of my cranium. It wasn't even that bad of a practice. I was still with the fourth liners but we had a good scrimmage and Terry's forward skating and slap shot continued to improve. His skating was still choppy, but he didn't fall down half as much as he used to. Best of all, Coach Brantford was pretty easy on me as this practice, Frankie was his whipping boy and I even got out of puck-picking-up duty.

Walking out of the locker room I was feeling pretty good, actually the best I had felt in a while. I heard someone shouting my name and looked behind me and Nick, the Zamboni driver was waving his arms and shouting my name. He came over quickly and said, "You have a phone call. You can take it back there in the office."

I walked into the office and picked up the phone and said hello.

"Tom, it's mom. Listen, I have some bad news. Your dad was in a car accident on the way to pick you up. The police told me that an elderly gentleman apparently had a heart attack and his car crossed the median strip on Johnson Boulevard and hit dad's car. I just got the call a few minutes ago," she said quickly.

I took a very deep breath and asked, "Well, how is he? Is he going to be okay?"

"The policeman I spoke to said he didn't know how he was," she said. "He told me he was being taken by ambulance to St. Mary Memorial. So, here's what we're going to do. I'm going to drive to the hospital right now. I called Mr. Barclay and he's going to pick you up at the rink and then drive you to the hospital and I'll be waiting for you in the Emergency Room. Okay, Tom?"

I didn't say a word and then my mom said loudly, "Tom, did you hear what I said? Mr. Barclay—"

"I'm sorry, mom," I said slowly. "I heard you. I'll wait for Mr. Barclay out front and I'll see you in the Emergency Room."

"Okay, Tom. I'll see you there," she said before hanging up.

I hung the phone up and sat at the end of the desk. Nick came in and asked me if everything was okay. I mumbled, "No...um, my dad's been in a car accident...and it's all my fault."

Chapter 16
Results

As I was standing outside, a few of the guys passed by and said goodbye to me. I didn't act like anything was the matter. Terry had left before me with his dad or I would have told him what had happened, but I definitely didn't want to mention it to anyone else. I was feeling unhinged deep inside because I was to blame for him being in the accident. Even though he was hit by a guy who had suffered a heart attack, he wouldn't have had to come back to pick me up if I hadn't started that argument with him. He would have stayed to watch a little of the practice and not been out on the roads.

"Tom, what are you still doing here?" Coach Brantford asked me as he came out of the rink. He was with Coach Malone. "You still waiting for your dad?"

"Well, um, I was actually waiting for our next door neighbor, Mr. Barclay, to pick me up," I said as I stammered and stuttered. "We're um, having some car troubles."

"Really?" Coach Malone chimed in. "I waved to your dad on my way in here."

"Yeah, well, apparently there was some kind of problem. I don't know what," I said.

Coach Brantford looked me over closely, as if he knew I was trying to hide something. He then said, "Tom, are you *sure* everything's okay?"

I took a deep breath and looking at my shoes said, "No, uh...my mom called and told me that my dad was in a car accident on the way here. A senior citizen had a heart attack and his car crossed the median on Johnson Boulevard and he plowed into my dad's car. My mom didn't know what kind of shape my dad was in. He's over at St. Mary's."

"Do you need us to do anything, Tom?" Coach Brantford said in a very serious tone.

"No, um, Mr. Barclay should be here soon and he'll drive me to the hospital. My mom is on her way there now."

"Let me get my gear home and then I'll head over to the hospital, too. It's not that far from my house," Coach Brantford said.

"Okay, Coach," I said quietly. A car then flashed its high beams and I noticed through the driving rain that it was Mr. Barclay's white Cadillac. Slinging my hockey gear over my shoulder I said to Coach Brantford, "I guess I'll see you there, Coach Brantford."

"I'll see you there, Tom. Tom..." Coach Brantford said as he looked me straight in the eye.

"Yes, Coach."

"Hang in there," he said in a reassuring tone. "Everything's going to be okay with your dad."

They went to their cars and I walked over to Mr. Barclay's Cadillac. As I was walking, the gale force winds blew the rain into my face. The high winds scared me but what was more scary was what was going on at that exact moment over at Emergency Room at St Mary's. Was dad even alive at this point? If so, what was the damage and how severe was it?

About all Mr. Barclay said on the ride over to St. Mary's was that he was sorry to hear about my dad and that he'd get me to the hospital as quickly as he could. He parked in the lot that was next to the Emergency Room and he walked with me into the Emergency Room waiting room. We saw my mom as soon as we walked in and she came running over.

"Thank you so very much for bringing Tom here, Mr. Barclay," mom said as she bent down to give me a tight hug.

"It was no problem, Mrs. Leonard," he said. "You two take care and let me know when you hear anything or if you need anything."

"So, what happened? Did you talk to a doctor yet?" I asked mom frantically.

"Look, it's going to be okay," mom said calmly. "The paramedic told me that your father was responsive. He said his left leg hurt a lot and he had some facial cuts. He said he'll be fine. He said our car was a mess but that it could have been worse. The older gentleman that hit him suffered a heart attack and he passed away."

"Dad's going to be okay?" I asked.

"It looks that way," she said reassuringly.

Mom was holding me tight and I didn't say what had happened. I didn't know if dad had told her or not. Mom held onto me until she heard her name being called. She shot right up and a guy with blue scrubs came over towards us.

"Mrs. Leonard?" he asked.

"Yes, I'm Alice Leonard and this is my son, Tom," she said.

"I'm Dr. Roesser," he said as he put his right hand out for mom and me to shake. "Well, the good news is that your husband is going to be fine. He's suffered some fairly serious injuries...he has a broken rib, a broken left kneecap and some lacerations to the face, chest and arm."

"Can we please see him?" mom asked.

"Sure, but just for a few minutes," he said. "One of the nurses will let you know when it's alright to come back."

We sat back down and the minutes passed like hours. I kept looking up at the big clock and it was like being in class at the end of the day when you are wishing it was 3:10 but it is 3:01, then 3:02 and then 3:04 and 3:10 just realistically seemed like it would never, ever arrive.

"You seem awfully, quiet," mom whispered to me. "Are you sure you're going to be okay to see your father? He'll probably be hooked up to a few different machines."

"No, I'm okay," I mumbled. "I just really want to talk to him."

"Well, hopefully in a few minutes," she said as she brushed my hair back with her right hand.

"Mom," I said slowly and quietly, "did dad tell you what happened in the car on the way to practice?" I asked.

She nodded her head and said, "He mentioned that you two had a talk about the way things have gone and that you weren't happy with the way the coach has been treating you. He did tell me that. Why are you asking?"

"He didn't say that we had an argument?" I said as I sat up straighter.

"No, he didn't say it was an argument," she said.

"Well, he was being too kind to me," I said.

"Why? How so?" she asked.

"I yelled at him, mom," I said looking down. "I yelled at him and I wouldn't listen to a word he was saying. I told him that I didn't want to grow up and be like him or Granddad. Mom, the things I said to him. I'm *such* a moron."

"Tom, I'm sure he knows you didn't mean that," she said as she grabbed both of my shoulders.

"Before practice I should have called you guys, talked to him, told him I was sorry for what I said," I said with my chin buried in my chest. "I should have called, I could have apologized and asked him to come and watch some of the practice and then he wouldn't have been on the road when that guy hit him. I could have done *something*!"

"No!" she said in a loud tone.

"Yes," I said as I started to cry. "He could have died and it would have been all my fault."

"Tom," she said quietly as she hugged me very tightly. The tears were streaming down both sides of my face.

"Mrs. Leonard? Alice Leonard? You can see your husband now. Room 159, straight through those doors, last room at the end of the hallway on the right," the nurse said.

Mom thanked the nurse and we walked through the large doors which had lots of warnings printed on them, and then we made our way back to dad's room. As we walked down the hallway, I started to look into the rooms, and saw people with tubes and wires coming out of them and at that point I knew it was best to just look straight ahead and put blinders up on both sides. I furiously wiped my eyes so that dad wouldn't know that I was crying.

Finally, we made it down to the end of the hallway to dad's room. Mom rushed inside but I took it a lot slower. I saw his legs and then, slowly, peered around the corner. I almost gasped for air as he was a mess. His face was cut up and puffy, his left arm was bandaged up and he had a tubes going into his right nostril and his right arm. Mom was holding onto him tight and Dr. Roesser, who was in the room along with a nurse, asked mom to be gentle with dad. He said something about how dad's been through a lot tonight. I wanted to tell him if he only knew the half of it.

I shifted around, behind mom, so dad could see me and he lit up a little when we made eye contact. I painted a smile on my face and said, "Hi buddy" to him and he very deliberately said, "Hi buddy" back to me. He then told mom about the accident as he said he saw the other driver coming across the median in slow motion and he was able to avoid getting hit head-on. Dr. Roesser told us that we'd have to leave as they needed to do more tests and also let dad rest. Mom gave him one last hug and told him that she loved him and would see him tomorrow as soon as they'd let her into the room to be with him. I stepped up to him and dad reached with his right hand and grabbed my left arm.

"Tom, I'm going to be fine," he said slowly.

"I know, dad," I said looking away from him. "It's just that those things I said about you and Granddad. I'm really sorry, I didn't mean them."

"I….know. It's okay…" he said.

"No, it's not," I pleaded with him. "I should have called and told you to come to practice. Better yet, I shouldn't have picked an argument with you. I was so wrong about everything…"

"Just remember," he said haltingly as his right hand fell to the bed. "Remember what your Granddad used to say 'gotta keep fighting, never stop.' Words that he lived by. I don't want to be an embarrassment to you...I always wanted to be a hero to you," he said as he reached up with his right hand.

I held his right hand tightly with my right hand and with tears welling up in my eyes I said, "You're not an embarrassment. You *are* a hero…*my* hero"

"I'm sorry, your father needs to get some rest," Dr. Roesser chimed in.

"I love you, dad," I said as I continued to hold his right hand tightly. I then placed it back on his bed and I leaned down and kissed his forehead.

Chapter 17
Recede
(Not Going To)

Dad ended up spending five days in the hospital and he spent about a week at home. At the end of that week, I think my mom was ready to break the kneecap that wasn't already broken and probably a few other bones too. See, while my dad might be the nicest and most gracious man on the planet, he may also be its worst patient. He constantly needed a glass of water or his pillows fluffed or new reading material. Plus, the phone calls! It's like his office couldn't get along without him. Mom was happy he was recovering, but she may also have been just as happy when he finally went back to work.

The next practice we had went okay. We worked mostly on drills and I was paired up with Terry and I worked a bit with John Rowan too. Still, no luck cracking the top two. Coach Brantford was riding me about making quick decisions, but the problem was that I was making the decisions *too* quickly as opposed to not making them quickly enough. I was going to explain to him that I was working at a speed, unfortunately, that I was accustomed to and the other guys on the third and fourth units weren't. I'd send the breakout passes out a half second too early and while Stevie or Frankie would catch the pass and be off to the races, those same passes to slower skaters or lesser skilled guys like Reese or Kelly simply clanged off their skates or hit them on the tape and they couldn't properly accept the pass.

None of that really mattered. The honest truth was that I was happy to be on the ice and what my dad had said on the ride to practice the night he was in the accident, finally sunk in. It wasn't important who I was playing with, just that I was playing. That he was okay, meant everything. To think that if things had been ever so slightly different, he could be dead now was a real good slap in the face for me. It felt like a second chance and I was going to take full advantage of it.

Coach Brantford showed me something too. After we left dad's room and were headed back to the car, we ran into him in the Emergency Room waiting area. He told me he came as fast as he could as he wanted to be there for me. He asked about dad and said he would have come back to the room, but the nurse said that only family members could see dad. He walked out to the parking lot with me and said that if we needed anything to call him as soon as possible. He even called our house after dad was back home and spoke with him for a few minutes.

Terry's dad drove him and me to the next practice and then our first exhibition game which was at Fairview the following night. We were playing Winston in the exhibition game and our first regular season game was against Lynnwood. Dad was hoping to make the Winston game but he said if he didn't feel up to it, then he would definitely be at the Lynnwood game.

It worked out good that he wasn't at the exhibition game. We were winning five to two with about three minutes to go and Coach Brantford called for Terry to play with Billy as Tim took a four minute roughing penalty. He went in, elbows high, into the corner and caught one of their guys pretty good. It had been a pretty chippy game to start with and Tim's penalty ratcheted things up about four notches. I was happy that Terry was going to go in as it would be his first penalty kill opportunity since he played on the team.

The face-off was in our end and the puck came back to Billy who sent the puck around the boards and all of the way down to the Winston end where their goalie stopped it. Our two forwards and their two defensemen raced after the puck. I looked back in our zone as their number 20 started jawing with Billy. Suddenly, he puts a bear hug on Billy and then does this WWF-style takedown and starts pushing his head into the ice.

Terry, in his inimitable skating style, comes over and grabs number 20 and tries to pull him off Billy. He was only marginally successful before their number 29 and their number 15 grabbed Terry and threw him to the ice. Number 20 saw those two standing over Terry and he got up and skated over and, as Terry was laying on the ice, started to drag him by the jersey. I yelled for Billy to get over there and help Terry but he just got up slowly and adjusted his pads. Meanwhile, Terry had a guy dragging him around and two other guys were taking swings at him. I yelled again for Billy to get over there, but he just watched what was happening to Terry.

Finally, the refs came over and broke the whole thing up and they threw the three Winston players right off the ice. Terry came over and sat down and I asked him how he was and he said he was okay. He looked a little woozy. I leaned down and said to Billy, "What happened out there?" He didn't answer me.

Once we got in the locker room, as I was getting out of my equipment, I asked Terry if he was sure he was okay. He said he was and he told me he was only trying to help Billy out. I told him I knew that and I was going to talk to Billy about it. I had only taken my shoulders pads off, my skates were still on, as I walked over to where Billy was getting undressed. He sat between Tim and Scott.

"What happened at the end there, Billy?" I asked him.

"Nothing, I don't know what you're talking about, Leonard," he said as he looked at Tim.

"Well, Terry, got that number 20 off of you and then the two other goons attack him, 20 is dragging him around like a bag full of trash and you had to make sure that hair 178 was still in place," I said. "So, why didn't you stick up for him?"

"I dunno," he said before he started chuckling with Tim.

"It's not funny," I said in a serious tone. "He helped you out, stuck up for you and you didn't do anything for him. You know, he is your teammate."

"He's a guy on this team, a friend of yours…so what," he said as he pointed a rolled up ball of black tape at me. Standing up he said, "Don't you dare talk to me about standing up for teammates after you left this team last year. You're such a hypocrite. You run up to play for some Canadian team and then you get cut. Don't lecture me, punk!"

"You and me, if we ever play together you can pull that gutless routine, but you pull that again if you play with Terry, I'll be right back here," I said looking Billy straight in the eye.

"Oh, me so scared," he said with a laugh. "It's too bad we can't cut you like that Canada team did, you know. Once the season gets going, that screw-up friend of yours isn't going to see the ice."

I could take his garbage about Canada but once he laid into Terry in front of the guys on the team, I knew I had to take a stand and just like Terry stuck up for him, now it was my turn to stick up for Terry.

"What you know about playing in Canada, could fit in a thimble!" I shouted as I grabbed Billy by the shoulders and pushed him into the wall. "That screw up sitting over there, he's forgotten more about hockey than you'll *EVER* know."

The room was silent and Tim and Scott each stood up quickly and looked as if they were going to try and separate me and Billy. Before they could start pulling us apart, Coach Brantford, who was standing at the opposite end of the room, yelled, "Let them go!"

"You blew it, dude," Billy said through clenched teeth. "You had a shot and *you blew it*!"

"I didn't blow it," I said as I grabbed his shirt as tightly as I could. "It was taken away from me."

"You didn't deserve it, I should have got the invite! Not you!" he yelled. "I could have gone somewhere, done something. You, you got options. Me…it's hockey or nothing. No scholarship, no college!"

"You have options," I said as I loosened my grip on his shirt.

"Yeah, like what? Work in the mill like my old man? Those jobs are gone, man. All the old man does is drink beer all day and talk about the past, and every now and then tells me I'm a loser and slaps me around. Wanna see his handiwork?" he spit out as he turned around and lifted up his shirt revealing red welts or bruises that looked like they came from a belt, going up and down his back.

I released my grip on his shirt completely and then dropped my fists of rage. I looked him in the eyes and then turned and saw everyone staring at us. I thought about offering Billy a handshake and say sorry or let's let bygones be bygones, but instead I just walked away. What can you say when someone says their dad drinks all day and then for fun, slaps him around and calls him a loser. Once again, my issues and problems were put in perspective. Not getting enough playing time or feeling that I was making a contribution to the team just didn't equate with suffering the emotional and physical scars that Billy had endured at home. Billy was an obnoxious jerk but the reasons for his 'jerkdom' became very apparent after our little dance that day.

Not that we were going to go out and hang out at the mall or send Valentine's Day cards to one another but that scuffle somehow brought Billy and me together a little bit. At a minimum, it helped us understand each other better. I was glad that the coach let us see it through to a conclusion instead of breaking it up. It did help me earn some much needed respect in the locker room, especially since I ended up riding the bench for the first fifteen games. Only an occasional shift and those usually came when the game was out of hand or on the power play. The team was doing great, our record was 14 and 1 and my rationale was that Coach Brantford didn't want to fix what wasn't broken.

Terry's early season improvement kind of fizzled out. He didn't have a point during the year and he was trying *so* hard to get that elusive goal. He actually came close when he and I got in at the end of the Butler game. With about a minute to go there was a face-off to the left of Butler's goalie and Reese won it cleanly and sent the puck back to Terry at the right point. Terry wound up and let a slap-shot go and it made it through a lot of traffic in front of the goal and the goalie kicked his right skate out to try and make the save but he missed the puck. As it got past him it looked like it was going to go in but it hit off the post and the goalie was able to recover the rebound with his glove. It was so close...

We had a great group of fans and they always filled up Fairview and when Terry came on the ice, they would chant "Ter-ry, Ter-ry, Ter-ry" hoping he'd get on the score sheet. He told me how great it made him feel when they chanted his name and I tried as best I could, in the limited time I played, to try and get him a point, but it just didn't work out for him. He never let it affect him, as he was the definition of a team player. We'd sit on the bench and he'd tell me about each player on the opposite team, what their weaknesses were. After a few shots on the opposition goalie, he knew where he was weakest and between periods he'd tell Coach Malone who was smart enough to listen to him. Coach Malone would then tell Coach Brantford and he'd pass the info onto the top two lines like it was his info. "Whatever," Terry would say, "as long as we win the coach can take credit for it."

We won our last three regular season games and then got by the Stockton Wings and the Lynnwood Knights in the playoffs and it came down to us and the Colts Hill Crusaders for the league championship.

Chapter 18
Resurrection

We played the Lynnwood game on a Saturday night and the league championship final game was scheduled for Sunday night, so there was no time to rest. Not that it mattered for me as I hardly played during the season and I only got a little power play action in the two playoff games. My stats were pretty low, three goals and six assists. Still, dad told me that he was more proud of my nine points this year, than the 64 I had the last year.

Life and hockey sometime take interesting turns and the hours leading up to the league championship final could only be termed interesting. I think Coach Brantford had another word in mind as he stood at the top of the steps at Fairview rink about an hour before game time.

"What's up Coach," I said as my dad and I saw him on our way into the rink.

"We got a problem…Mr. Leonard, can you suit up tonight?" he asked dad.

"If I have to suit up, you've got *real* problems, coach," dad said with a laugh.

"Well, we have got a real, real big problem. We may have only nine players tonight. There must be a stomach virus going through the locker room or at the schools because I got calls all afternoon from parents saying that their kids were throwing up all morning," he said.

"Right now we'll have five forwards, three defensemen and one goalie. It's bad…even against a weak team we'd have a hard time competing, but to go against Colts Hill… well…"

"We're going to play, though, right Coach?" I asked in a serious tone.

"As long as we have nine, I guess we can go out there," he said. "There's Coach Simpson, let me go over and talk to him."

Dad and I walked in and I headed to the locker room. In there were Steve, Frankie, Bobby R., Brian, Billy, Larry, Reese and Terry. Collectively and individually, they looked scared so my guess is that they already knew the news about our lack of manpower.

"Who died?" I said as I sat down next to Terry.

"The Magic Rats," Frankie said.

I got dressed and as I was taping up my shin guards, Coach Brantford came into the room and quickly came over to me and told me to step outside for a second.

"Yes coach," I said as we stood outside the locker room.

"Come here," he said as he motioned for us to go into a corner. "Tom, I know this year hasn't been easy with the lack of playing time and, of course, your dad's accident. I've made it very difficult on you. I've tried to be consistent and at the beginning of the year, I was punishing you because you went up to play in Canada. I didn't play you because I wanted to punish you for missing the last three games last year. I also wanted to prove to the team, and you and even to myself that we could win without you. It was terribly unfair of me to do that to you and I apologize."

"Apology accepted, Coach," I said matter-of-factly. "Can I go back in and get ready?"

"Look, Tom," he said very slowly, "we only have nine, they have 21. We've got Brad, I mean, Brian in net. We have Stevie up front. I just don't want to get humiliated. Believe me, Simpson will rub our noses in it."

"Why are you telling me this, Coach?" I asked.

"I'm going to need you to play, virtually, the entire game. It's going to be you and Billy and I know you two have had your issues. I can work Terry in here and there and call our time outs and talk to the refs to slow the game down. Can you play most of, if not the whole, game?" he asked.

"Well, I am pretty well rested," I said with a laugh. The coach looked too embarrassed to laugh but, looking down at the ground, he did just that. "I'm ready to rock and roll and I think those guys in there are too," I said as I pointed toward the locker room.

"No one would blame you if you didn't go full tilt, tonight," the coach said.

"Do you need me now?"

"I do."

"Then I'm in, 150 percent," I said. "I do have one question. Last year, at the practice where I told you I was going to accept the invite to play for the Red Raiders in Canada—"

"Yeah?" he asked.

"I saw you, Coach Malone and Billy talking and afterwards Billy took several runs at me. My thought was that you made Billy take those runs at me. True or false?" I asked him.

"False. Billy came up to me and Coach Malone and asked me if I approved of him taking runs at you. I told him that I don't condone thuggery and that he would have to let his conscience be his guide," he said without blinking.

"I also saw you talking to him after practice," I said.

"If you would have hung around after practice, you would have received an apology from Billy for the cheap shots. He came up and told us that he wanted to send a message to you and to the team. I told him that his behavior was unacceptable and I told him that he should go out and apologize to you after he did 50 pushups and 100 sit ups," he said. "When he was done with those, you had already left the rink."

"I just thought maybe, you know…you put a bounty out on me or something," I said sheepishly.

"A bounty…that's really, really funny! Where'd you come up with that idea? I know, when you were up in Canada you must have watched Don Cherry on Coach's Corner, right?" he asked and then started to laugh.

"Maybe…once or twice," I said softly.

He slapped me on the back a few times and we walked back to the locker room. Before we walked in I looked back at him and said, "You know, coach…this one's for friendship." He paused for a second and then nodded and we walked into the room. The guys were all ready, the ones that were here, that is.

"Okay, guys listen up," Coach Brantford said. "You know where we're at. We have nine healthy players and they have their full team, ready to go. I was talking to their coach and that jerk thinks they won the championship already. He's telling them that they were already the better team and now with so many of our players out, they'll walk to 12 or 15 goals against us!" He continued loudly, "I want to tell you guys, with or without our other players, I know for a fact that I am in the room with the best team.

The team with more heart and more guts. We're going to have Steve, Tom and Billy play almost the entire game. I want Bobby R. to start with Steve and Frankie upfront. Whenever anyone is tired, dump the puck in and change them up. Ice the puck, freeze it along the boards anything to chew up some time and shorten the game. Terry, you'll play defense when Billy and Tom need a quick rest and you may have to play forward as well. I want you ready at all times. Brian, all I can say to you is do everything in your power to stop the puck. We'll need you to also freeze the puck at every opportunity so we can change up the lines and give everyone a chance to rest. Forwards, do not, I repeat do not skate the puck in. When you get over the red line, dump the puck and wait for them to come to us. Got it? Okay, one last thing. You need to promise me, and promise each other, that you will each give no less then 150 percent effort tonight. I'm asking you to give each other everything you've got and then give some more. You'll need to defend our goal, maybe take a hit, a punch or whatever it is those guys dish out. We may not come out of this victorious, but I know when the game ends, that each of you will be able to look me in the eye and say that you did your best. You can say to your family and friends, and someday your own kids or grandkids that for one night, for one game your teammates, your blood brothers and you, shared a common goal of doing your absolute best under very harsh conditions. Win or lose, you made a vow, no retreat, no surrender. Okay, let's go!!!!!"

It was a great speech, we were all ready to punch holes in the wall we were so fired up. It was the us against the world mindset that the coach mentioned and we were feeding off it. As we stepped on the ice, the crowd, seeing that we only had nine players, cheered, whistled and roared so loudly that my ears hurt.

As Stevie lined up for the face-off, Billy skated over to me, tapped his stick against my shin pads and said, "Ya' feeling, okay?" and I tapped my stick against his shin pads and said, "Never better."

Chapter 19
Rise Up

The game started out fast and furious. The Crusaders were doing their best to run us out of the building as quickly as they could. This was good strategy considering we only had three guys on the bench at any given time. We weathered the storm early and Coach Brantford wisely took a timeout with six minutes to go in the first period. Brian was playing good, he was like the Flash in that he was pushing himself from side to side and throwing his body around to block shots so quickly. He also had two associate goalies in me and Billy. We would each stand on the side of the net and we each took a few shots in the gut and off the shins.

We were executing the game plan, dumping the puck and basically keeping all five guys back on our side of the red line. I was conserving my energy and I felt good enough that I didn't have to take a break. Finally, with 38.4 seconds left in the first period, I came off the ice. Billy stayed on and Reese joined him on defense. Reese, Larry and Billy had played a lot as Steve and Bobby R. were getting a little fatigued. The Crusaders were keeping their shifts short and they ran four lines against us to wear us down. As the whistle blew to end the first period, their strategy was working.

The first two minutes of the second period, it became like a shooting gallery. The Crusaders had at least ten shots on goal and probably ten more that weren't on goal. Brian was amazing. We picked up the play a bit, Larry and Frankie were all over the place trying to pick up Steve, Billy and me. Again, with six minutes to go in the second period and still no score, Coach Brantford called a timeout.

"Alright, you guys are doing great but we have to try something," he said. "They're easing up a bit because you guys are taking their best punches. Now, you go on the attack. Reese, you drop back on defense with Billy, Tom you move up to forward with Steve and Frankie. You guys are going to have one shot to go for it. The face-off is in their zone. Steve, you have to win the draw and then Frankie you line up just outside the crease and try to screen the goalie. Everyone else, just throw as many shots as you can at their goalie. Terry told me that he noticed in warm up that he is weak on his skates and on his stick-side. Alright, let's go!"

I was glad that we were going to go for it. If we wanted to win, eventually we'd have to score a goal and now with the face-off in their end, the time seemed right. Steve won the face-off and drew the puck back to Billy. In what seemed like an eternity, Billy lined up the puck and did his usual routine of throwing his whole body into the shot and I watched the puck fly off his stick towards the goal. Frankie was battling one of their defensemen in front and the puck, which was coming in high, hit off the back of his helmet and laid there on the ice in the upper slot. Steve swung around one of their players and whipped a wrist shot to the goalie's stick side and then everyone heard a loud ping as the puck hit off the post. It was behind the goalie who couldn't see it and Frankie and I lunged to swat it into the net. The referee blew his whistle and pointed to the net as the puck was over the line! The goalie had put it in his own net accidentally! The crowd, which was 95 percent Magic Rats supporters, went ballistic. They were clapping and stomping and the old barn was literally shaking.

After we celebrated the goal, Coach Brantford huddled us up and told us to drop back into our defensive shell. I looked over at the Crusader bench and a bunch of their guys were slumped over and shaking their heads and to me that was a great sign. They were like the boxer who's given his weaker opponent everything he could handle and still no knockout.

The defensive shell worked for the rest of the period. They only got about four shots and Billy and I were sending pucks flying left and right, trying to clear the zone. We were able to get a little bit of a rest as the Zamboni would clean the ice between the second and third period. In the locker room, Coach Brantford urged us to hold the fort, simply get the puck and clear it out. Play smart, don't take any penalties and we would be the league champs. We were all so fired up after scoring that goal. It was at that point that we now believed we not only could win, but *should* win!

As soon as the third period started, I became distracted looking at the clock, wishing it would say '0:00'. Instead, it moved very slowly which was in direct contrast to the Crusaders who were back to running four lines. It was like standing in the ocean and waiting for the waves to crash into you. They were back to throwing everything at us, and this time with desperation. Collectively as a team by the ten minute mark, we were pretty well spent physically. Even Reese, Larry and Terry were tired. Billy and I were simply standing by the sides of the goal as we could barely move.

The Crusaders took around 18 shots on us and between Billy, myself and Brian we stopped them all. With about four minutes to go, the crowd, who had been loud consistently throughout the game, turned the noise up a notch which gave us a little energy boost. They were banging the glass, stomping their feet and cheering each time we cleared the puck out of our zone.

With two minutes, I looked around and really thought we had it! The crowd was screaming and all we had to do was keep dumping it out of the zone and basically put all five guys around the net. Coach Brantford took our final time out and echoed those thoughts. Billy, Bobby R., Frankie, myself and Steve were on the ice since about the five minute mark and we were, literally, working off of fumes. As we came out for the face-off, which was in our zone, Steve raised his arms to the crowd and exhorted them to cheer even louder. I wasn't even sure how he had the energy to raise his arms at that point.

Perhaps he used his last bit of energy, because their center beat him cleanly on the draw and he picked up the puck and walked in on Brian all alone. It was a move Mario Lemieux used to do and Billy skated over and tackled him which drew a penalty. It was our first penalty of the game. Billy shook his head but it was a penalty, no doubt. Terry came out to replace Billy on defense. The Crusaders took a time out.

After the time out the same center took the draw against Steve. He drew the puck back to the point this time. The defenseman wound up and let a slap shot go and Brian somehow made the first stop. The puck was sitting on the doorstep and Terry took a swing at it and missed it. It squirted to the left side of the net and I dove to try and cover it for a face-off. One of the Crusaders beat me by a half a second and took a shot which Brian stopped but the rebound came out and the Crusaders center got the perfect carom and he had a wide open net to shoot at and BANG, it was in the back of the net. Just like that, the Crusaders had tied the score with 1:09 to play.

The crowd had been standing for most of the game, suddenly sat down. You could feel the disappointment as we were only 69 seconds from shutting them out. Now, they had all of the momentum and we could barely stand up, let alone skate and try and score a goal. Coach Brantford huddled us before the face-off at center and told us not to give up. Our body language, though, told the story. Plus, we all could have used some oxygen. I spoke up and said, "We can still do this!"

After the draw the Crusaders shot the puck in and I corralled it near the left circle. I passed the puck over to Billy and he passed it right back to me. The Crusaders forwards and defense were hanging back at the blue line waiting for me to come out. So I held the puck and took a quick look at the clock. I had started up the ice and I heard Coach Simpson yell, "NOW!" and the three forwards started tearing into our end, all three skating right at me.

This surprised Billy, Steve and Frankie who used what little energy they had to try and catch them. Bobby R. fell down near the bench and then I saw him get off the ice. The two Crusader defensemen moved forward and then they started skating at me too.

I didn't panic, I circled back and then went behind the net. I looked up and saw all five Crusaders coming at me, I figured I'd just skate it, or try to skate it, right through them. Out of the corner of my eye I saw Terry step on the ice. He was all alone at the red line as all five of the Crusaders were coming at me and they didn't see him step on the ice. If I could get the puck to him he'd have a shot at a breakaway.

I was in the slot and just as the first wave of three Crusaders were about to crash into me and me into them, I did a Spin-o-rama and barely holding onto the puck I sent a back hand pass through the center of the ice, away from the second wave of Crusaders. The puck floated gingerly and almost magically right onto Terry's stick. He picked the puck up in front of the red line and it was him and the goalie, one-on-one with the clock ticking down.

Everyone watched as Terry, with his choppy, quick strides skated over the red line. The Crusader goalie didn't move. The crowd, rose as one and started screaming. It seemed like an eternity as Terry went over the blue line and then approached the slot. The Crusader goalie still didn't come out, instead hanging back near his goal. Terry held the puck out front and then raised his stick up slightly, banged his stick to the right and then to the left as the goalie took the fake and lunged forward with his stick to try and poke check the puck away. He missed it and was now out of position. Terry transferred the puck to his backhand and then in a split-second backhanded the puck into the open net for a GOAL!!!! He crashed into the boards behind the goal as he couldn't stop in time.

Chapter 20
Redemption
(Part 2)

The sound was again deafening as we raced to the Crusader end to celebrate with Terry as the clock read 0:04.19. For that brief moment in time, Terry was Wayne Gretzky, Mario Lemieux, Rocket Richard, Gordie Howe and Bobby Orr all rolled into one. The moves were insane, the results a dream come true and the best part of what had just happened was the way the crowd cheered.

Even though there were 300 people there and we were in a little barn-like rink in East Slade, PA, it felt as if we were in an NHL rink with 20,000 people and we had just won the seventh game of the Stanley Cup in overtime. The crowd and the team came together as one and it was an incredibly powerful moment.

I skated up to the hero and yelled, "You did it! One goal, you wanted to score one goal and it just so happens that it was the best goal I've ever seen!"

"Couldn't have happened without you," Terry yelled back. "Just like we drew it up on the bench." We hugged and then skated to the bench.

Our two coaches each gave Terry a bear hug and Bobby R. and Reese were punching him so hard on the shoulders I thought the impact would send his helmet flying off. The ref dropped the puck and the 04.19 seconds ticked off and we were the champions! We skated over to Brian, who could have been the co-MVP of the game with Terry, to hug him and then we lined up to shake hands with the Crusaders. I watched as even bitter enemies Coach Simpson and Coach Brantford shook hands. The crowd continued shouting and cheering and I skated over to where my mom and dad were and gave them a thumbs up. Even though I was incredibly tired, the adrenaline was running upstream against the fatigue at that point.

The commissioner of the league then came out with the championship trophy. It wasn't the Stanley Cup but it was a nice sized trophy and he gave it to Billy. Billy then skated it over to me. It was a classy move but I wasn't the guy who should be the first to skate around the rink with it. That honor belonged to the hero of the game, Terry.

I gave him the trophy and said, "You're the reason we won. You deserve to take it first." He smiled and said thanks and, choppy skating and all, took the first lap around with the trophy. The song "Best of Times" by Styx was playing over the PA but you could barely hear it as the crowd chanted in unison "Ter-ry, Ter-ry, Ter-ry." He came over to me after his lap and I said, "Do one more," and he laughed and went around again, this time backwards, to even louder cheers.

We went on to win the state championship (with our full team by the way) but I think we all remember the league championship a bit more fondly. Burned into my memory are the faces, the faces in the crowd, the guys on our team and Coach Brantford too. When I think about it, I am still amazed by the fact that everyone came together. The team, the crowd, we were all living in that moment and that feeling of being one…that's what sports should be about.

Bruce Springsteen once talked about being "in concert" with the crowd and when those special moments happen and fans and team or fans and performer are *in concert* together, it's pure magic. And that night 20 years ago was just that, pure magic.

Chapter 21
(My Beautiful) Reward

So, today was the team reunion and most of the guys were supposed to be attending. We were playing the game at the old barn and then having a meal at a restaurant that Reese's family had owned and operated in town for 40 years. A lot the guys have families of their own now and have moved out of the area, so it will be nice to see them.

Playing in the reunion game with those guys will be a lot of fun. A good portion of the Magic Rats went on to play for the East Slade High School team and in my junior year we finished third in the state of Pennsylvania. In college, I played on the school's club team and on weekends I played in pick up games with some of the older guys in town. I still play once or twice a month in pick-up games, although now I'm the old guy as I play against guys who are half my age.

Some of us never left beautiful East Slade. A few of the guys like Billy, Frankie and two of the Bobby's I see once in a while. Terry, well I see him everyday. After he graduated from Carnegie Mellon University, he worked for a software company in California. About five years ago we were talking on the phone and I told him that the owner of Fairview was selling the rink and he, excitedly, said we should buy it.

"As your accountant (having graduated from Robert Morris University with an accounting degree, I was working for a CPA firm at that time) it's a risky move due to the condition of the rink and the capital that would need to be invested in it. Although, as your best friend, I say let's do it!"

We each quit our jobs and now we own the rink. We refurbished it to bring it into the 21st century and we renamed it the De-Lo Arena in honor of our dads and Granddads. We took the first initial of our dad's middle names and the first initial of our Grandad's first names and came up with the name De-Lo.

Terry helps run things and he also teaches at Carnegie Mellon part-time and I oversee the business and hockey side of the rink. I also coach an adult amputee team and a youth sled hockey team. Both of whom have amazing athletes who prove to me day in and day out what hockey is all about.

My dad was right when he said that, "One day you'll fly." Although neither of us could have predicted that I would fly to places such as Riga, Latvia and Elista, Russia. I went to Riga with my adult amputee team and Elista with my sled team to play in tournaments. I even took my dad on the Elista trip and joked with him about his famous comment about flying. He said he meant it figuratively that I would fly and I told him that he was, as always, right.

I was talking at the rink one time with the dad of a kid who was interested in playing sled hockey. We started talking about playing hockey and he was worried how his son would react if he didn't do well or fit in with the other kids. I paused and then remembered back to a conversation that I had with Terry when we were growing up. I smiled and then said to the dad,

"I'm sure your son will be fine and enjoy his time playing hockey on our team. The point is, and I learned this a long time ago before I could let other things into my life...to have the opportunity and the chance to play hockey, anywhere at anytime meant the world to me. To be playing the game with my friends on the ice, in a parking lot or in someone's backyard or basement whether it was in the dead of winter or on a warm summer's night, it made me feel alive and it gave me the idea that I could do *anything* if I put my mind to it and worked hard enough. It nourished my soul and fed my brain. I am a hockey player for life, by being involved with the game, I hope your son one day will grow up to be one too."

12396954R00080

Made in the USA
Lexington, KY
08 December 2011